Before Sabrina could get settled in her classroom, her cell phone rang. She fished the phone out of her bag and answered in a whisper. "Why are you ringing? I turned you off!"

"This is a wake-up call," the phone said in a dull tone.

"I'm awake," Sabrina said, still whispering. She pushed Off and put the phone aside.

The instant Sabrina picked up her pen, the phone rang again. This time she was sure she had turned off the phone.

Her teacher, Mrs. Chadwick, set her book aside and stood up. Sabrina pointed the phone out of the classroom and into her bedroom. It could ring there all day and not bother anyone but Salem.

"Is there a problem, Sabrina?" Mrs. Chadwick asked.

"No, uh—wrong number. I just got my new cell phone and I haven't figured out all the buttons yet."

The phone popped into her bag and rang again.

Panicking, Sabrina grabbed the phone. "Hello?"

"This is a wake-up call."

"What?" Gasping, Sabrina slapped her hand over the mouthpiece and looked at her teacher with genuine shock. "Uh—family emergency! Gotta go!"

Grabbing her books and bag, Sabrina fled from the classroom without waiting for permission. She was the desperate owner of a cell phone that wouldn't shut up or stay put.

Titles in Sabrina, the Teenage Witch® Pocket Books series:

All Pocket Book titles are available by post from:
Simon & Schuster Cash Sales, P.O. Box 29, Douglas, Isle of Man IM99 1BQ
Credit cards accepted. Please telephone 01624 836000,
Fax 01624 670923, Internet http://www.bookpost.co.uk
or email: bookshop@enterprise.net for details

Sabrina The Teenage Witch®

Wake-Up Call

Diana G. Gallagher

Based upon the characters in Archie Comics

**And based upon the television series
Sabrina, The Teenage Witch
Created for television by Neil Scovell
Developed for television by Jonathan Schmock**

POCKET
BOOKS

LONDON · SYDNEY · NEW YORK · TOKYO · SINGAPORE · TORONTO

POCKET
B O O K S

An imprint of Simon & Schuster UK Ltd
Africa House, 64-78 Kingsway
London WC2B 6AH

Copyright © 2001 Viacom International Inc.
All rights reserved.
POCKET BOOKS and colophon are registered
trademarks of Simon & Schuster

A CIP catalogue record for this book is
available from the British Library

ISBN 0 7434 0419 X

1 3 5 7 9 10 8 6 4 2

Printed by Omnia Books Ltd, Glasgow

With affection for Rebecca Mariani, one of my best friends back home in New York

Wake-Up Call

Chapter 1

☆

Sabrina strapped on her watch quickly and reached for her books. As she did, the early morning light glinted on the watch face. "*Seven*-fifteen!" Sabrina exclaimed. "Wait a minute . . ." She paused.

"What time did you think it was?" Salem smoothed back his whiskers with a damp paw.

"Eight-fifteen. It should be eight-fifteen. My clock alarm went off at seven-fifteen and I've been up for an—" Sabrina picked up the clock and shook it. Then she saw the date. "April first."

"It's April already!" Salem exclaimed.

"As if you didn't know." Sabrina crossed her arms and glared at the cat. The look of wide-eyed innocence on his furry, black face didn't fool her for a second. "You reset my alarm clock, Salem."

"Me?" Salem stiffened and planted a paw on his chest. "Now *why* would I do that?"

"Because it's April Fools' Day!"

1

"Oh, yeah." Salem chuckled. "Sorry. I couldn't resist."

"How hard did you try?" Sabrina asked. Somehow, she couldn't picture the cat struggling to overcome his mischievous nature.

"Not very. Starving cats are not prone to overlooking the perfect opportunity to make someone else miserable." Salem sighed. "Are you mad?"

"I should be, but—no." Sabrina shrugged. She had gotten off easy. Last year Salem had convinced her that Aunt Hilda and Aunt Zelda were planning to ship her off to boarding school. *And it almost worked because he convinced* them *that I wanted to go! Like I'd willingly trade cool clothes and Harvey for blue blazers, kneesocks and no boys on campus,* she thought with a shudder.

"So—what are you going to do to get even?" Salem winced.

"Nothing." Sighing, Sabrina sat down beside him.

"Nothing?" The cat scowled. "Witch's honor?"

Sabrina yawned loudly and held up her hand. "Witch's honor. So I lost an hour's sleep. No biggie, except I'm not used to having time to kill before school. What do people do at seven o'clock in the morning?"

Salem grinned. "They watch happy, snappy morning news shows on TV and stuff themselves with Bavarian cream doughnuts."

"Bavarian cream?" Sabrina gave the cat a curious once-over. "Does that mean you're not going to win your bet with Aunt Hilda?"

"Wanna bet?" asked Salem. He flexed a front paw. "I've been working out and no feline will be able to resist me."

Sabrina rolled her eyes. The vet had said that Salem could lose two pounds to be in optimal health, and so Salem had bet Aunt Hilda that he would lose two pounds in two weeks so she wouldn't switch him over to nasty-tasting diet cat food. Of course, if Salem won, Hilda had to feed him anything he wanted for a month. If Salem lost, he had to stick to dry diet kibble without complaining for a month. Judging from the look on his face, his exercise program was going very, very well.

Sabrina's stomach grumbled.

"Bavarian cream doughnut?" Sabrina asked.

"Not interested," sniffed Salem. He flopped onto his stomach and stretched happily. "I've lost the two pounds, but I don't have an ounce to spare!"

"That's wonderful, Salem! To be honest, I didn't think you could do it."

Salem groaned. "Oh the sacrifice! My thighs hurt from my last workout. Hmmm . . ." he said. "What could one doughnut hurt? Point up a doughnut for me!"

"Forget it. You've got less than eleven hours to go."

"Easy for you to say," Salem huffed. "You haven't been running up and down the stairs and playing with stupid kitty toys for exercise for fourteen days. All for my health." Salem sighed and blinked at Sabrina.

"Yeah right," she said. "Who are you trying to impress?"

"That Persian who moved in down the block looks mighty fine," responded Salem. "In fact, I see candlelight and catnip for two in her future." Salem waggled his whiskers.

A date, Sabrina thought. Harvey popped into her head and her gaze settled on the phone. She sat up and smiled. "Brilliant idea."

"What?" Salem's ears perked forward.

"Let's give Harvey a wake-up call!" Grinning, Sabrina picked up the phone, but her finger froze over the buttons when she heard Aunt Hilda's voice on the line. She sounded perturbed.

"I know it's not even seven-thirty yet, Mr. Browne," Hilda said. "If you had returned my calls yesterday and the day before that, I wouldn't be calling at this uncouth hour."

Sabrina replaced the receiver and threw up her hands. "This day is not getting off to a great start. Why did Aunt Hilda have to use the phone the *one* morning I've got time to call Harvey before school?"

"Not a disaster. Maybe Hilda and Zelda will give you your cell phone early—"

"Cell phone?" Sabrina interrupted.

Salem slapped his paws over his mouth.

"Did you just say my aunts were giving me a cell phone, Salem?"

"Cell phone? No!" Salem shook his head. "I said, uh—*spell cone.* Yeah! It, uh, amplifies spells—like

4

a megaphone for magic. No witch should be without one."

Sabrina raised her finger. "Do I have to use a truth whammy?"

"Me and my big mouth," Salem muttered.

"Yes! I'll finally be connected to the world by wireless!" Sabrina dashed out the door.

"Please, don't tell Hilda and Zelda I told you," the cat called after her. "It's supposed to be a surprise!"

I'm surprised! Sabrina thought as she skidded to a halt at the top of the stairs. *Not to mention ecstatic and relieved.* She was absolutely certain she and Gordy were the only kids in the senior class who didn't have a cell phone on them at all times. *And Harvey. Of course, Gordy and Harvey don't care that being cell phone-less is totally last millennium.*

She had been begging her aunts to get her a cell phone for weeks.

Can I help it if I'm shallow and overly image conscious? she thought. Taking a deep breath, Sabrina walked down the stairs.

Hilda walked through the front foyer and stopped dead when she saw her niece. "What are you doing up so early?"

"Salem was just having some annoying feline fun this morning," Sabrina said, leading the way into the kitchen. There they found that Aunt Zelda was up, too. She was working on the household accounting. From the look on her face she wasn't happy with what the calculator read.

"Thank goodness." Hilda collapsed in a chair

across from Aunt Zelda at the table. "For a moment I thought my clock was wrong. And if my clock was wrong, then 314 other clocks in the shop are wrong, too."

"I'm glad you're up early, Sabrina." Aunt Zelda set down her cup of tea and turned off the calculator.

"You can thank Salem." Sabrina dropped her things by the door and sat down. "Where is he?" asked Hilda.

"He's been avoiding the kitchen ever since he made that bet with you," Zelda said.

"Does he look skinnier to you?" Hilda asked.

"Yep, but not thin enough to indulge his sweet tooth." Sabrina pointed up a Bavarian cream doughnut with chocolate frosting.

Hilda and Zelda both gave Sabrina a stern look as she bit into the doughnut.

"What?" Sabrina asked.

"We have something serious to discuss with you, Sabrina." Sighing, Zelda sipped her tea.

Sabrina quickly stuffed her mouth with doughnut to hide a smile. *Very clever,* she thought. *They're obviously pretending something's wrong as an April Fools' joke before they give me my cell phone.*

Zelda reached for one of the papers on the table and held it in front of Sabrina's face.

Uh-oh. Sabrina winced when she recognized the monthly phone bill. Last month she had promised to cut back on her long-distance calls. *And I did,* she assured herself. *I only called Aunt Vesta twice when she was on safari in Africa.*

"Who do you know in Afghanistan?" Zelda asked.

"Nobody." Sabrina put her doughnut down and pointed up a glass of O.J. "That was a wrong number. I meant to dial Dad. He's back in Paris on vacation."

"Twenty-two dollars for a wrong number?" Hilda sputtered.

"Well, the woman who answered didn't speak much English and it took forever to make her understand I dialed her by mistake," Sabrina said.

"Why didn't you just hang up?" Zelda asked.

"I didn't want to be rude," Sabrina explained defensively.

Zelda rolled her eyes, then scanned the bill. "Did you know your average phone call to Val lasts four hours and thirteen minutes?"

"It does?" Sabrina didn't keep track. Before Valerie had moved to Alaska with her family, she had been Sabrina's best friend for two years at Westbridge High. Dreama, her new best friend, was nice and fun for a witch with a chronic misfiring spell problem, but she was from the Other Realm and not totally tuned in to mortal girl problems. *Besides, I miss Val.*

"Even at five cents a minute that's over twelve dollars a call—four or five times a week!" Hilda threw up her hands.

"Care to take a guess how much it costs to call Gwen in London?" Hilda leveled Sabrina with a stony stare.

Sabrina shook her head. She and Gwen, another witch with a spell-accuracy deficiency, had gotten to know each other in Italy and saw each other on vacation when they could. *Which isn't very often,* Sabrina mused. "How much?"

"Three dollars a minute." Zelda shook the bill. "It would be cheaper to just pop across the Atlantic if you want to chitchat with Gwen for hours in the middle of the night."

Sabrina started. "Are you giving me permission to pop around the world whenever I want?"

"No!" Hilda picked up a pencil and tapped it on the table. "We're revoking your long-distance privileges until you pay your bill."

Sabrina stared. "Aren't you taking this joke a little too far?"

"Three hundred and forty-two dollars in long-distance telephone calls is not a joking matter, Sabrina." Zelda put the bill back on the table.

"See?" Hilda made a scowling face. "I'm not laughing."

"You guys are good." Sabrina grinned, convinced they were putting her on. "Okay, where is it?"

Hilda and Zelda exchanged a glance.

"Where's what?" Hilda asked.

"My new cell phone." Sabrina leaned forward expectantly.

"What cell phone?" Zelda's eyes narrowed.

"The one Salem said—" Sabrina looked toward the door when she heard the cat chuckle.

"Gotcha!" Salem collapsed in a fit of laughter. "I love April Fools' Day!"

Chapter 2

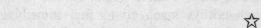

"Three hundred and forty-two dollars." Muttering, Sabrina sank onto her bed in a state of shock. She had seventeen dollars in the bank and another five in cash until payday at the coffeehouse.

"Okay, so that's another sixty after taxes," she calculated out loud. "Subtract my weekly expenses, factor in a fifty-cent tip per coffee customer, and—I won't get that bill paid until Christmas!"

Sabrina fell back and threw her arm over her eyes. She absolutely could *not* survive without long distance! If she didn't talk to Val every other day, they wouldn't stay best friends for long. The last time she called, Val had spent most of the conversation gushing about Helen, her new lab partner. *How cool can a walking chemistry textbook be?*

"What I need is five minutes of Gwen therapy." Sitting up, Sabrina exhaled. Her own problems always seemed petty compared to the disasters that plagued Gwen. "It's a little hard to stay bummed about a few split ends when Gwen accidentally turns her hair into steel wool with a magic perm point."

A smile tugged at the corner of Sabrina's mouth. Calamity was Gwen's middle name, but the perky, British witch always managed to find something funny about the disasters that plagued her. *Like wondering if steel hair will rust if she washes it,* Sabrina thought with a glance at the phone, which she couldn't use to call outside Westbridge, which only made her feel worse!

The Bavarian cream doughnut settled like a rock in Sabrina's stomach, and beads of cold sweat broke out on her brow.

"Great! I'm going into long-distance withdrawal!" Upset and annoyed, Sabrina rubbed her pointing finger, which was itching to dial. A cell phone would have taken the sting out of being cut off from global gossip. But now, thanks to Salem's April Fools' joke, she missed not having a cell phone a hundred times more than she had before!

"Robbing me of an hour's sleep is one thing. Building my hopes up about a cell phone I'm not going to get is another." Sabrina stood up, her jaw set with resolve. "And that demands drastic retaliation."

Sabrina drew a blank as she marched down the hall to the bathroom to brush her teeth. She wanted revenge with something awful, but harmless, that would drive the cat crazy for a day.

Sabrina thought as she squeezed toothpaste onto

her brush. She glanced down at the bathroom scale and grinned, remembering her earlier conversation with the newly buffed cat.

"I've lost the two pounds, but I don't have an ounce to spare!"

"Not an ounce to spare, huh? Perfect." With a quick point, Sabrina adjusted the scale to weigh the cat half a pound heavier than he actually was. She didn't want Salem to lose his bet with Aunt Hilda, but it wouldn't hurt him to spend the day *thinking* he was going to lose! "One despicable April Fools' joke deserves another."

Back in her room, Sabrina's thoughts immediately turned back to her communications crisis. The only thing worse than being a high school senior without a cell phone was being in college without one. Changing her student status from being on top of the high school heap to being a lowly freshman on campus would be hard enough without the added burden of being an uncool, technology-deprived, lowly freshman. She couldn't even save to buy her own cell phone now that she had to pay her long-distance bill.

"Some days it just doesn't pay to get up." Sighing, Sabrina reached for her books and straightened suddenly. "I'm a witch! Since I can't afford a cash-and-carry cell phone from Totally Talk at the mall, maybe I can get a *point*-and-carry cell phone from the Other Realm!"

Pulling her magic book out from under her bed, Sabrina flipped to the index. There was no category for telephone, so she turned to the page for inter-realm communications. The listing for Witch Wireless seemed more promising than Point 'n' Prattle or Magic Messenger.

"New customers, please point to activate the acquisition department." Crossing then uncrossing her fingers, Sabrina took a deep breath and pointed.

A stream of smoke appeared and slowly coalesced into a short, slim, matronly elf wearing a tailored business suit, green shoes with curled, pointed toes, glasses, and a black nametag with Nancy printed in gold. "Good morning! Welcome to Witch Wireless. Are you ready to sign on the dotted line?"

"That depends." Sabrina was startled when a pink paper contract and a quill pen materialized in Nancy's small hands. "Is Witch Wireless a cell phone service, and how much does it cost?"

"Yes and nothing!" Nancy spoke with a lilt and giggled. The contract and pen were left dangling by her shoulders when she spread her arms and opened her hands to emphasize her point.

"Nothing?" Sabrina eyed the jovial elf with suspicion. Everything had a price, especially Other Realm products. Magical "bargains" always had hidden costs that weren't measured in dollars and cents. *Such as running shoes that have to be exercised five miles a day or they howl all night,* she recalled with a grimace.

"Not a dime!" Nancy patted a few stray, gray hairs back into the tight bun at the nape of her neck. "Not with our fabulous introductory offer!"

"Okay, I'm listening." Sabrina perched on the

edge of her bed and folded her arms. An introductory offer sounded good, but she didn't want to get her hopes up just to be disappointed again.

"Excellent!" Nancy shooed the hovering contract and pen off to the side. A slim, compact cell phone popped into her palm when she snapped her fingers. "This nifty little model is called the Silver Cloud SDE—Super Deluxe Edition. It has point-and-touch tone dialing, voice-activated information service, an unbelievable range of many, many mortal miles, plus wake-up call at no additional charge."

Wake-up call sounds like a handy feature, Sabrina thought. She could set the phone to go off instead of her alarm and have a Salem-proof wake-up call! "Does it come in other colors?"

"No, but it's all yours at *no* cost for a one-week free trial! Full service to anywhere in this world or the other one included," Nancy finished.

"What happens at the end of the week?" Sabrina asked, her eyes narrowing. If Nancy noticed her reluctance to believe the sales pitch, she didn't show it.

"Well, you can either sign up to extend service at a reasonable rate or you can give the phone back with no further obligation." Shrugging, Nancy flicked her wrist with a flourish. The phone vanished into thin air.

"Wait!" Sabrina jumped up, thinking the phone was gone for good. "Did I flunk the new customer gullibility requirements or what?"

"No, dear. I just thought you might want a closer

look." Nancy snapped her fingers, and the compact cell phone popped into Sabrina's hand.

"Too cool! And so small!" Sabrina flipped the phone open and stared at the golden numerals and letters embossed on a smooth, silver touch pad. The itch in her dialing finger intensified. "Can I take it for a test call?"

"By all means. You have five minutes to decide before your eligibility for the introductory offer expires." Nancy waved and popped out. The contract and pen stayed behind.

"Five minutes?" Sabrina protested. "I'm a teenager! I can't make a phone call that only lasts *five* minutes!"

"Four minutes and forty-five seconds," Nancy's voice cooed. "And counting."

Sabrina punched in Harvey's number.

"Yeah?" A gruff voice answered.

"Mr. Kinkle? Sorry to call so early, but it's really important. Is Harvey there?"

"No Harvey here, lady."

Sabrina flinched when the phone went dead. She had called Harvey ten thousand times! How could she get a wrong number? Hoping it wasn't a weird glitch in the phone, she paid closer attention to the small touch pad when she dialed Harvey again.

A muffled voice answered on the second ring. "Hello?"

"Is that you, Harvey?" Sabrina tensed. "Because it doesn't sound like you."

"Sabrina? What—"

"Hi, Harvey!" Sabrina interrupted. "For a minute there I thought there was something wrong with my new cell phone. Well, it's not exactly mine. I haven't closed the deal yet." She spoke in a rush and waved the contract and feathered pen away when they zoomed in.

"What time is it?" Harvey's drowsy voice suddenly sounded frantic. "Am I late?"

"No, you've got half an hour," Sabrina assured him, "but I've only got two more minutes and fleeting seconds! Do I sound like I'm speaking from an echo chamber or anything?"

"What are you doing in an echo chamber at eight o'clock in the morning?"

"I'm not *in* an echo chamber. I just want to know if I *sound* like I am because"– Sabrina paused when the pen tapped her on the shoulder and pointed at the clock—"never mind, Harvey! I'll explain when I see you at school."

Hanging up, Sabrina dropped the phone on the bed and grabbed the contract and pen. "Okay, where do I sign?"

"Right on the dotted line," Nancy said as she popped back in. She stood on tiptoe to watch as Sabrina put pen to paper and quickly scrawled her name.

I hope I'm not going to regret this, Sabrina thought as she handed the pink paper to the elf. She glanced at the sleek, silver cell phone on the bed and promptly dismissed her anxieties. *Free trial for a week? No obligation? How can I go wrong?*

"Congratulations! If you have any problems, just call customer service!" Nancy folded the contract, jammed the pen into her bun, and disappeared.

"Okay. Done deal." Sabrina picked up the phone, dialed the clock shop, and hit Send. She couldn't shake the feeling that Nancy had pulled a fast one. *Maybe I should have read the contract before I signed it,* Sabrina thought as the Clock Shop answering machine picked up.

"If you're looking for a clock, you've called the right place," Aunt Hilda's voice said. "Right place, wrong time. Our hours are Monday through—"

"It really works!" Hanging up, Sabrina tucked the phone into her bag, grabbed her books, and raced downstairs. Aunt Hilda and Aunt Zelda were still sitting at the kitchen table, but now they were going over the clock shop accounts.

"Did Mr. Browne *say* he'd come pick up those watches today?" Zelda asked.

"Not exactly," Hilda replied with a pained expression. "He reminded me that we got them at a ridiculously low price because there isn't a return policy."

"What are we going to do with thirty-six watches that have a thirteen o'clock?" Zelda looked appalled.

"Well, we could slow down the planet so it takes twenty-six hours to rotate instead of twenty-four," Hilda suggested.

"Great idea!" said Sabrina. "Then you'll have a jump on the new market!"

"No can do." Zelda sighed. "No magic for personal profit."

"I'm glad to see you're in a better mood, Sabrina," Hilda said. "What gives?"

"You didn't try to get a loan from Morton's Easy Magic-Cash to pay your phone bill, did you?" Zelda's expression was poised between disappointment and relief. "At his interest rates, you'll lose your powers for a couple centuries."

"Nope! No loan!" Sabrina smiled tightly. She couldn't decide whether to tell her aunts about the terrific deal she had gotten on the cell phone or not.

"Good." Hilda sagged. "Because there's no law against running a scam in the Other Realm."

"How else could anyone get away with selling 13-hour watches?" Zelda chimed in. Hilda shot a narrowed glance at Zelda.

"We'll figure something out, Hilda." Zelda smiled at Sabrina. "One of these days you'll thank us for making you take responsibility for your actions and paying your own long-distance bill."

"You are so right," Sabrina agreed, grateful for the change of subject. "I'll see if Josh can give me some extra hours."

"That's the spirit!" Zelda raised an encouraging fist. "If you want, you can work off some of your debt helping us with inventory this week."

"I'll check my schedule. Gotta go." Sabrina waved and hurried out the door. No way she was going to tell her aunts about her new Witch Wireless cell phone. If there was a catch, she didn't want to know.

Chapter 3

Salem waited thirty seconds after Sabrina left before he came out of hiding. She had forgiven him for changing the time on her alarm clock—a decoy prank to put her off-guard—but he didn't think she'd be so quick to forget the cell phone joke.

Out of sight, out of mind, Salem thought as he padded out from behind the buffet in the dining room. He had scored a major April Fools' hit. Rubbing it in would have forced Sabrina to get even. "I had a good laugh. Why tempt fate?"

The tantalizing scent of freshly baked doughnuts wafted from the kitchen. Salem's stomach grumbled and his mouth watered, but all that exercise was paying off. That cute Siamese at the book store had given him the once over, and he wasn't going to give in to that temptation, either. Feeling virtuous, he padded into the living room and jumped onto the couch just as Hilda and Zelda entered the room.

"This is the second month in a row the Clock Shop expenses have been twice as high as the profits, Hilda." Zelda's tone reeked of exasperation. "And now on top of everything else, we've got a thousand dollars' worth of worthless watches we probably can't give away! We won't stay in business long if this keeps up."

Hilda looked suitably guilty for a split second, then grinned. "That's it! We'll give them away!"

"There's a brilliant moneymaking scheme," Salem said.

"I can do without the sarcasm, Salem," Hilda scowled.

"He's got a point." Zelda straightened a crooked picture with a point, then flopped in the armchair. "How would that help?"

"Couldn't we write it off as a PR expense?" Hilda picked up the cat and sat down. Instead of setting him down, she held him up and jiggled him, testing his weight. "You *do* feel lighter, Salem."

"Hey! I'm a cat, not a yo-yo!" Salem squirmed out of her hands and dashed to the far end of the couch.

Zelda nodded thoughtfully. "Actually, a PR promotion might work. It won't help pay the bills this month, but a write-off will certainly help with next year's taxes."

"Good! Now can we talk about something else?" Hilda pointed. A plate of crab-stuffed mushrooms appeared in her hand, which she shoved under Salem's nose. "Mushroom?"

Salem immediately went into gastric shock. His

stomach knotted and saliva dripped from his fangs. His mind shut out everything but the juicy pink bits of crabmeat nestled in plump brown mushrooms glazed with melted butter. He leaned forward, jaws open—and sank his teeth into thin air.

What? Salem blinked.

"Hilda!" Zelda stood by the coffee table holding the plate, which she had snatched away. "He's only got seven hours to go!"

"I know." Hilda glared at Zelda. "And if Salem wins the bet, it'll cost a small fortune to feed him for the next month. Bye-bye budget."

"We haven't started rationing our magic yet," Zelda countered.

Salem stared at the mushrooms. They were only a pounce away. One big jump, a swipe of his paw, and one of those gourmet morsels would be his. *Crouch, twitch, ready—no!*

Executing an about-face, Salem bolted out of the room, up the stairs, and into the bathroom. He had pushed the envelope of his willpower to its absolute limit. With the aroma of sautéed mushrooms permeating the whole house, he needed a progress fix to resist. He stepped on the scale.

"Seven hours and counting. I can do it. I know I"—Salem gasped when he saw the digital readout—"*gained* half a pound!"

Stricken, Salem dragged himself to the bath mat. This wasn't possible. He hadn't eaten anything since he had weighed himself at five o'clock that morning!

"Oh, no!" He'd promised Trinket, the gorgeous Persian, tons of caviar and steak tartare on the assumption that he'd win his bet with Hilda and Zelda and they'd have to order him up feast after feast. Now she would never go to the monthly Alley Cat Screech and Howl Midnight Social with him.

Even after getting up an hour early, Sabrina arrived at Westbridge High later than usual. After dumping her afternoon books in her locker, she risked breaking Mr. Kraft's speed limit and raced through the school at a jog. She took her seat in first-period English a minute before the bell rang.

Made it, Sabrina thought with relief. The only bummer was that she had missed the before-school gab fest in the halls. Now she'd have to wait until lunch to show off her new cell phone. *Except nobody knows I've got it so I won't get any calls!* She didn't want to be obvious about flaunting the sleek, silver phone, but that problem was easily solved. *I'll just think up a reason to call my aunts at the clock shop.*

"Hi, Sabrina!" Cheryl Scranton leaned forward in her seat behind Sabrina. "What's new?"

"Cell phone!" Grinning, Sabrina pulled the Silver Cloud SDE from her bag and held it up.

"It's silver." Cheryl recoiled slightly, as though the phone threatened to mute the vibrant pinks and greens in her plaid blazer.

"What else?" Sabrina's cheeks flushed with indignation. A silver cell phone wasn't her first choice, either—but it was better than no cell phone.

And the price was certainly right! She leaned toward Cheryl, matching the other girl's subtle look of disdain. "Silver is the *only* color now that retro's back in."

"It is?" Cheryl frowned, puzzled.

"Totally. Besides, gold would look tacky on crimson or chartreuse, don't you think?" Sabrina flipped the phone open to show off the embossed touch pad.

"Oh, absolutely. I'm trading in my Blue Babble tomorrow." Cheryl nodded and picked up her pen. "What's your number?"

"Uh—" Sabrina stalled. She had forgotten to ask Nancy, and the phone hadn't come with instructions. "What's my number?"

The cell phone rang.

Surprised, Sabrina fumbled the phone, recovered her cool, and touched Send. "Hello?"

"Your number is 555–2324," a voice said in a robotic monotone.

"Who is this?" Sabrina asked, jotting down the number.

"This is Silver Cloud SDE information," the phone replied.

"We're ready whenever you are, Sabrina," Mrs. Chadwick said from the front of the room. She silenced a ripple of muffled laughter with a stern frown.

"I'm ready!" Sabrina turned the phone off and shoved it back in her bag. She wasn't sure if the Silver Cloud SDE answered only phone-related questions or if it would respond to *any* question. But since questions were a given in every class, she didn't want to risk having a know-it-all phone con-fiscated.

"All right, then." Squaring her broad shoulders, the portly Mrs. Chadwick picked up her copy of *Classic Short Stories,* which was required reading for all Westbridge seniors. "Those of you who didn't finish last night's reading assignment have fifteen minutes to speed-read it now. The rest of you can begin answering the questions at the end of the selection."

Sabrina had read the assignment and flipped to the questions. She was grateful for the head start on to-morrow's homework, because she had to work after school. *Now I'll have more time to talk to Val and Gwen when I get home! And it won't cost me a cent.*

Before Sabrina finished reading the first ques-tion, her cell phone rang. She cast a nervous glance at Mrs. Chadwick and averted her gaze when the teacher frowned. She fished the phone out of her bag and answered in a whisper. "Why are you ring-ing? I turned you off!"

"This is a wake-up call," the phone said in the same dull tone.

"I'm awake," Sabrina said, still whispering. She disconnected and studied the touch pad, wondering if she had hit the wrong button before. She pushed Off and set the phone aside.

The instant Sabrina picked up her pen, the phone rang again. This time she was sure she had turned the phone off. Was this a deliberate malfunction she should have expected in an Other Realm product, or had the phone been preset to a wake-up time by the manufacturer? Either way, she was in trouble.

Mrs. Chadwick set her book aside and stood up.

Sabrina pointed the phone out of the classroom and into her bedroom. It could ring there all day and not bother anyone but Salem. *I can pop home to call customer service during lunch.*

"Is there a problem, Sabrina?" Mrs. Chadwick asked.

"No, uh—wrong number! I just got my new cell phone and I haven't figured out all the buttons yet. You know how complicated high tech can be. It's turned off now." Sabrina noted that every head in the class turned toward her. *Score!*

The phone popped back into her bag and rang again.

Sabrina stared. The Silver Cloud SDE obviously had some magical properties Nancy hadn't told her about.

Rolling her eyes, Mrs. Chadwick headed toward Sabrina's desk.

Panicking, Sabrina grabbed the phone. She couldn't let the teacher take possession of the Other Realm device. There was no telling how the phone would react, and she couldn't ignore the possibility it might cause a major upheaval in the magic-mortal continuum. "Hello?"

"This is a wake-up call."

"What?" Gasping, Sabrina slapped her hand over the mouthpiece and looked at the teacher in genuine shock. "Uh—family emergency! Gotta go!"

Grabbing her books and bag, Sabrina fled from the room without waiting for permission. This was an emergency of the worst kind. She was now the desperate owner of a cell phone that wouldn't shut up or stay put!

Sabrina ran for the rest room, hoping that customer service at Witch Wireless had a quick, easy fix. The phone's repeating message echoed through the empty halls.

"This is a wake-up call. This is a wake-up call."

Sabrina dashed through the rest room door, locked herself in a stall, and shouted at the phone. "What part of 'I'm awake' don't you understand?"

Chapter 4

In order to call customer service, Sabrina had to get the number from the cell phone's information feature. However, that required a clear line, which she couldn't get. Every time she disconnected, the phone rang back repeating the wake-up call before she could ask a question.

"No wonder the Silver Cloud SDE is free for a week. It's basically useless!"

Since she couldn't go back to class until the phone was fixed, Sabrina popped home to get help. She had no intention of asking her aunts, because she wasn't in the mood for a lecture. If she had consulted them first, they would have warned her about the bugs in the Witch Wireless phone system and reminded her that nobody gets anything for nothing.

"Except a whole lot of trouble." Dropping her books and the nagging phone on her bed, Sabrina consulted the magic book. The number for customer service was listed in the Witch Wireless ad.

Sabrina picked up the phone and wiggled her dialing finger to loosen it up. Then she hit Off, Send, and the first numeral of the service number in quick succession.

The phone rang.

Throwing up her hands in frustration, Sabrina tossed the phone back on the bed and let it ring. She turned back to the book, but there was no listing for repair. Out of ideas and patience, she pointed for the new customer department. That morning it had summoned Nancy. Now, she got an instant message. The six-inch, neon green letters hung in midair in the middle of her room.

You are already a Witch Wireless customer.
Please call customer service.

"I can't call customer service because your stupid phone is stuck in a wake-up loop!"

The instant message dissipated into a green haze that smelled faintly of mint.

Sabrina sat in a daze. *My life has been put on hold by a phone!* She couldn't stash it in space where no one could hear it ring because it would just come back. She couldn't go to school or the coffeehouse, and she couldn't hide it from her aunts. They'd hear it the minute they walked in the door. Since she'd have to tell them about the cell phone anyway, she might as well get it over with. She couldn't even hope that the batteries might go dead, because the phone was powered by magic.

As Sabrina raised her finger to pop to the clock shop, a black blur zipped by the open door. *Salem?* The cat was just as informed as her aunts in matters of magical mishaps. *Maybe more so, since he's had a lot more experience trying to beat the system,* she thought.

Sabrina ran out into the hall just as Salem skidded to a stop, changed directions, and charged into the bathroom. She got to the door just before he slammed it closed.

"What's going on, Salem?" Sabrina pushed the door open and waved away the hot steam that billowed out of the small room. The ringing phone appeared in her hand. She tucked it behind her back.

"Close the door!" Panting, Salem sat on the edge of the tub. "You're letting my sauna escape!"

"Since when are you into taking steam baths?" Sabrina asked, raising her voice to be heard over the ringing.

"Since I gained half a pound in three hours." Sighing, Salem hung his head. His damp fur was matted to his body, and his sides heaved from being out of breath. The cat looked completely miserable. "I've been running and steaming. So far I've only lost one lousy ounce."

Sabrina wilted, not just from the hot mist but

also from regret. She hadn't expected Salem to go on a one-day crash diet and marathon exercise program. "You didn't gain any weight this morning, Salem. I changed the settings on the scale to get back at you for April Fools'."

"What? I can't hear you!" Salem wailed. "Now my ears are ringing!"

"Your ears are fine, Salem," Sabrina shouted. "This stupid phone won't stop—"

The ringing stopped.

"—ringing." Sabrina whipped the phone out from behind her back. Seconds passed and it remained silent. Why? She hadn't done anything, so she could only assume Witch Wireless had fixed a system glitch at their end.

"What's that?" Salem squinted through the fog that still rose from the hot water pouring out of the bathtub tap.

"Uh—you didn't gain weight this morning, Salem," Sabrina confessed again to distract him. She couldn't trust the cat to keep the phone a secret from Aunt Hilda and Aunt Zelda, especially on April Fools' Day. "I adjusted the scale so it would weigh you half a pound heavier."

"April Fool?" Salem asked.

Sabrina nodded and shrugged.

"Well, adjust it back!" The cat jumped onto the scale. "Now, if you don't mind."

Sabrina pointed at the scale, adding an ounce in Salem's favor to make up for his bad morning. "Gotta get back to school. Later, Salem."

As Sabrina dashed back to her room to get her things, Salem's voice rang through the house.

"Two ounces *under!* Wahoo!"

"Hey, Sabrina!" Harvey called out from down the hall. She grinned as he jogged up to her locker. "Where have you been all morning?"

"Well, to make a long story short—"

"I can't wait to hear," Mr. Kraft interrupted from behind her.

"Mr. Kraft!" Sabrina jumped and turned to face the principal.

"One of these days I'm going to write a book compiling the most creative and amusing excuses I've heard for skipping class." The withering force of Mr. Kraft's scowl diminished when he yawned.

"I, uh—had an emergency at home," Sabrina said. "The cat was sick."

"Close, but you'll have to do better than that to make the final edit." Mr. Kraft stifled another yawn. "Before you go on record, you should know that I called your aunt Zelda after Mrs. Chadwick reported your hasty departure and failure to return to English first period." His sly smile was chilling. "She doesn't know anything about an emergency."

"She doesn't?" Sabrina's eyes widened with mock innocence.

"How did you know the cat was sick if you were in class?" Harvey asked.

"Good question, Kinkle." Mr. Kraft stared at Sabrina, waiting for an answer.

"Well, he . . . I, uh—" Stumped, Sabrina hesitated. She couldn't think of a logical explanation other than a telepathic link with Salem. *Which might actually work,* she realized. After dating Aunt Hilda and then Aunt Zelda for over a year, he had learned to tolerate or ignore all the weird stuff that happened in the Spellman household.

"Mr. Kraft?" Harvey leaned in front of Sabrina and waved his hand in front of Mr. Kraft's face. The principal had fallen asleep leaning against the lockers. "He must be really tired."

"Apparently. So let's not wake him up." Grabbing Harvey's hand, Sabrina hustled him down the hall toward their next class.

"I'm glad I caught you before lunch," Harvey said. "There's something I've been meaning to ask you."

"Something good or something bad?" Sabrina asked.

"I won't know until I ask," Harvey said.

Sabrina stopped at the end of the corridor. This didn't sound like a something they could discuss in transit. "So ask."

"Well—" Harvey sighed and stared at his feet.

"What is it, Harvey? I hate suspense when I don't know how something's going to end."

"Well, I was just wondering if you'd mind if Brad went with us to the basketball game Friday night."

Sabrina tensed. "A double date?"

Harvey and Brad didn't know it, but Brad had been born a witch hunter. He could sense magic when it was used in his presence, and if he outed her as a witch, she'd be turned into a mouse for a hundred years. During the months since Harvey's old grade-school friend had returned to Westbridge, Sabrina had come way too close to giving herself away too many times.

"Not exactly." Harvey shuffled his feet. "He doesn't have a date. That's why he wants to go with us."

"Oh." Sabrina didn't know what to say. Spending too much time with Brad made her nervous, and acute anxiety made her more prone to making mistakes. *One reckless point and presto! I'll be the only rodent enrolled at John Adams College.*

"Bad idea, huh?" Harvey looked crestfallen.

"No, it's just that except for the actual state championship, the final play-off is the biggest game of the year! And I just, well—I really wanted to watch it with you, being us. *Just* us, you know?" Sabrina cringed at how selfish and insensitive she sounded, but she couldn't tell Harvey that his best friend was an unwitting agent of potential doom for her!

"Does that mean no?"

"No," Sabrina quickly clarified, but she tried to keep her enthusiasm to a minimum. "I mean, if Brad *really* wants to be the odd man out on our date, it's okay with me. It won't interfere with holding hands, will it?"

"Not a chance." Waving, Harvey walked back the way they had come to get to his next class.

As Sabrina turned the corner, she saw Brad cast a quick glance over his shoulder as he hurried away.

She felt a momentary twinge of remorse, then shook it off. If he *had* overheard her conversation with Harvey, it served him right for eavesdropping. Besides, she had agreed to let Brad ruin her date with Harvey.

Sabrina rushed through the cafeteria line, grabbing a gelled fruit salad and a soda. Harvey was already sitting at their usual table.

"That's not much of a lunch," Harvey said when Sabrina slid into the seat opposite him.

Sabrina's stomach churned as she eyed his tray: two milks, three pizza slices, a hot dog, chocolate pudding, and a slice of key lime pie.

"It's not like you have to watch your weight or anything." Harvey lifted the plate with the pie and offered it to her. "This is great."

"Thanks, but I'll stick with the low-fat, no problem diet." Sabrina shuddered at the thought of eating the portions Harvey ate. The last time she had tried a magic fad diet, she had disappeared—literally. *"Fade" diet would be more accurate,* she thought as she peeled the paper off her straw.

"You're sure?"

"Positive." Sabrina smiled tightly.

"Good." Harvey yanked the plate back and dug in. "This was the last piece."

Setting her soda aside, Sabrina casually reached into her bag and pulled out her new cell phone. She didn't want to look like she was showing off, so she just turned it on and put it by her tray without a word. With luck, Wireless Witch would call her to apologize for the wake-up call fiasco so she could answer it. That should draw some attention. At least the Silver Cloud SDE wasn't ringing incessantly.

Harvey polished off the pie and attacked his pizza. He smiled at her between bites, but he was oblivious to everything that couldn't be ingested.

What's the point of having a status symbol if nobody notices that you've got it! Sabrina's irritation mounted as she picked at her salad. Nobody was going to call her, so the only solution was for her to call out.

"Excuse me, Harvey." Sabrina picked up the phone. "I don't mean to be rude, but I really have to make this call."

"Okay." Harvey wiped his mouth with his napkin, opened a carton of milk, and chugged it.

Rolling her eyes, Sabrina dialed the clock shop. Aunt Zelda answered.

"What's going on, Sabrina?" Zelda asked. "I aged a century when Willard called about an emergency. If I hadn't called home and talked to Salem, I'd be frantic right now."

"What did Salem say?"

Harvey looked up sharply. "Doesn't he meow like other cats?"

"I meant *stray,*" Sabrina hissed.

"He said he couldn't get through to his diet crisis hot line counselor," Zelda said, "and you saved him from a day of unbearable torture starving in a sweat shop."

"That's close!" Sabrina cast a glance at Harvey, but he was focused on chocolate pudding. She turned away to sign off with her aunt. "All's well that ends well. I'll explain later. Bye!"

"Hey!" Harvey's voice rose above the din of conversation around them.

Finally! Harvey had noticed her phone! Sabrina mentally prepped herself to act like it was no big deal. Still holding it, she looked around with a smile that froze in place when Harvey waved Brad over to their table.

"Hi, Brad! Have a seat." Harvey picked up his second milk carton and shoved his tray aside. "Sabrina and I were just talking about you."

"But we weren't doing it on my new *cell* phone." Sabrina held up the silver phone, but the little electronic wonder didn't register with Harvey or Brad.

"We're all set for the game Friday night," Harvey said. "The three of us. Do you want to drive or should I beg my dad to let me borrow his car?"

"Actually, I've decided to stay home Friday night." Brad didn't sit down, and Sabrina had the distinct feeling he was avoiding eye contact with her.

"And miss the second biggest basketball game of the year?" Harvey was incredulous.

"Something came up." Brad shrugged and shifted his weight.

This certainly qualifies as an awkward moment. Sabrina was almost sure that Brad had heard her and Harvey talking about it earlier. *And he must have gotten the impression I really wasn't wild about the idea.*

"What could be more important than the play-offs?" Harvey asked.

Brad evaded the question. "I'll see you later, okay?"

Feeling rotten about making Brad feel rotten, Sabrina almost told Brad that she really did want him to go to the game with them, but she controlled the irrational compulsion. She was Harvey's girl-friend, and she was tired of competing with Brad for Harvey's time and attention.

"Bummer," Harvey mumbled as Brad walked away.

Sabrina's phone rang. Thrilled, she answered without giving a thought to the fact that no one she knew had her number except Cheryl. "Hello!"

"This is a wake-up call."

Sabrina stared at the phone, appalled. *Is it my imagination or does this phone sound smug?*

Chapter 5

Hilda unwrapped a new supply of credit card slips while she listened to Zelda's half of the conversation with Sabrina. Creepy Willard Kraft had upset both of them when he had called about an emergency.

The high school principal—Hilda's ex and the current love of Zelda's life—had had more than one head-on collision with a spell gone wrong, and he tended to overreact at the least little thing.

"Should we worry?" Hilda asked when Zelda hung up.

"I don't think so." Zelda leaned against the counter. "I have a feeling April Fools' Day had something to do with Salem's problem."

"Did Sabrina get him good?" Hilda's eyes lit up. "I still haven't decided how to get back at him for that prank he pulled on me in nineteen seventy-four."

Zelda giggled. "Sorry, Hilda, but decorating the

house like it was Halloween to make you think you had forgotten everything that happened for the previous six months was one of his more ingenious ideas."

Hilda forced a smile. "Almost as ingenious as the time he replaced all your clothes with larger sizes so you thought you were shrinking."

"Don't remind me!" Zelda pointed, and the sign on the door flipped so the OPEN side was facing the street. The three people who walked by didn't even glance at the window display. "Looks like it's going to be another dull day."

"Not if I can help it." Hilda straightened the stack of PR flyers that had just been delivered via Broomstick Parcel Express from Duplicates Done. The Other Realm company had charged an exorbitant amount to process the order, but she and Zelda had more magic in their Other Realm account than they had money in the mortal bank. "After I pass these out, business will boom."

"I hope you don't mean that literally." Zelda picked up one of the flyers. "Duplicates Done has never filled an order for the mortal world before. What if these flyers *do* blow up or something?"

"A magical booby trap?" Hilda studied the flyer and frowned. The information regarding their business hours and address was arranged above a realistic picture of an old-fashioned alarm clock. The "wacky-wrist-watch" giveaway announcement was underneath the picture. "Oops."

"Oops?" Zelda's face went white.

"This is supposed to say 'wacky-wrist-watch.' "

Zelda scanned the text again. "But it says 'a free wacky-*witch*-watch with every purchase'!"

"Well, that's better than having the flyers explode, isn't it? Besides," Hilda said as she walked to the door with the flyers, "thirteen-hour watches are *perfect* for Halloween!"

"But it's not Halloween," Zelda protested.

"April Fool! The customers will love it!" Hilda pointed a gotcha finger at Zelda and stepped outside to drum up some business.

"If we get any customers," Zelda muttered.

Sabrina dashed from the cafeteria and raced for the rest room with the phone ringing in her bag. She ran into Gordy as he rounded a corner with his nose in a book.

"Gordy! Just the person I needed to see!"

"Really?" Gordy looked pleasantly surprised for a second, then frowned. "Why?"

"Because I desperately need your help," Sabrina said. She had planned to finish her science report in the library during study hall next period, but, while her leather bag muted the sound of the ringing phone to a degree, it was not enough to meet the librarian's standards of acceptable noise levels.

"Whatever you need, I'm your guy, Sabrina."

"I need your science report." Sabrina didn't want to take advantage of Gordy, but he was probably the only kid in seventh-period science who wasn't scrambling to finish the assignment at the last minute.

"Don't think so. Sorry, Sabrina."

"But, but—I don't want to copy it! I just need to use it as a reference because I can't go to the library because I can't make this stupid phone stop ringing!" She hated getting hysterical in the halls, but her ability to remain calm had disintegrated twenty-four rings ago.

Gordy adjusted his thick glasses. "Why don't you just answer it?"

"Oh, well, there's a brilliant idea! Like that will help!" Sabrina had no sympathy when Gordy blinked in stunned bewilderment. *It's not like I planned to cheat,* she thought as she resumed her race to the rest room. Desperate circumstances demanded desperate measures.

Two freshman girls were primping at the mirror when Sabrina entered. They parted like a field of tall grass in the wake of a stampede when she moved between them. Fuming, she dropped her things on the sink counter.

The younger girls exchanged a glance. The shorter one cleared her throat. "Uh, excuse me, but—your phone's ringing."

"I'm not deaf," Sabrina huffed, her eyes flashing.

The intimidated girls ran for the door and the safety of the corridor.

Sabrina was immediately sorry she had taken her frustration out on them. She was even sorrier when the phone's ringer suddenly got louder. The shrill sound echoed in the large, tiled room. She finally answered it in self-defense.

"This is a wake-up call."

"This is a nightmare!" Sabrina shouted into the mouthpiece and disconnected. When the phone started ringing again, she dropped it on the floor and stomped on it.

"Is something wrong with your phone?" Dreama walked in and eyed Sabrina with unruffled curiosity.

"Yes!" Sabrina stopped trying to smash the insidious phone. It was undamaged, but the sole of her foot was bruised. "You're from the Other Realm, Dreama. What do you know about Witch Wireless cell phones?"

"You use them to make telephone calls?" Dreama asked uncertainly.

"Which is hard to do when it won't stop calling you," Sabrina quipped.

"Oh. I've never had a cell phone, so I wouldn't know." Dreama picked up the phone. "Why don't you just answer it?"

"Because I know what it's going to say." The tantrum had taken the edge off Sabrina's temper, but her nerves were shot. "It keeps getting stuck in wake-up call mode, and the ringing is driving me crazy!"

"Is that all? I can fix that." Dreama pointed at the phone.

The ringing stopped.

Sabrina was cautiously amazed. Dreama rarely

worked a spell that didn't have unusual and often disastrous consequences. "What did you do?"

"I cast a spell to mute it—" Dreama's words were drowned out when the phone suddenly blared like an emergency Klaxon.

"Reverse the spell, Dreama!" Sabrina shouted, but Dreama couldn't hear her over the blaring sound. Just as well, Sabrina decided on second thought. Another Dreama spell might have the phone ringing with sonic booms.

Sabrina grabbed the phone from Dreama. Just as she was about to pop home, Mr. Kraft barged through the door. "Mr. Kraft! This is the girls' room!"

"No. This is outrageous!" Mr. Kraft stood holding the door open, glaring at her.

Standing on the opposite side of the open door, Dreama waved at Sabrina and popped out of the combat zone.

In the hall, students were running for the exits. The phone's new and improved decibel levels had been mistaken for a fire drill.

"I'm not sure how," Sabrina shouted, "but I can explain!"

"Don't bother!" Mr. Kraft shouted back. "You're fired!"

"You can't fire me," Sabrina screamed. "I'm a student!"

"What? Oh, right." Mr. Kraft swayed slightly and rubbed his eyes. Then he spoke quickly between Klaxon rings. "You're suspended until further notice."

"Suspended?" Sabrina begged for mercy between the next two rings. "Can't we discuss this?"

"No!" The principal looked back as he turned to leave. "Now get out of my school and take that bellowing contraption with you!"

Sabrina winced. "Is that your final answer?"

Chapter 6

"Hit the deck! Every cat for himself!" When Sabrina popped in with the blaring phone, Salem leaped off the kitchen counter and took cover behind the trash container.

"Shut up!" Sabrina's books hit the floor with a sharp crack as she dropped them to grab the phone in both hands. The incessant ringing had her so unnerved that she heaved the Silver Cloud SDE against the wall. It bounced back into her hand. Giving up, she hit Send to silence the deafening ring.

"This is a wake-up call!" A distinct note of irritation had crept into the phone's voice.

Salem peeked through the paws covering his eyes. "Who's that?"

"This is a wake-up call!"

Sabrina clamped her hand over the speaker. "It's the phone."

"I *know* it's a phone." Salem's raised hackles bristled. "I may be a cat, but I'm not stupid."

"Unfortunately, I can't say the same for myself," Sabrina muttered.

"This is a wake-up call!"

Sabrina clamped her hands over the speaker.

"Oh-oh." The cat jumped back onto the counter and sat on an open package of cheese curls. "You fell for a Witch Wireless free trial offer, didn't you?"

"This is a wake-up call," the muffled voice said.

"How'd you guess?" Sabrina sank into a chair. The table was covered with half-eaten snacks. She shoved aside an empty anchovy tin, a bag of pretzels, and an unopened can of clam chowder with tiny teeth marks in the top. "You're jumping off the food wagon a little early, aren't you, Salem? It won't be six o'clock for another five hours."

"I couldn't help it!" Salem smiled and burped. "After steaming and running all morning, I almost passed out from hunger. Kibble just didn't cut it." He licked his stomach.

"This is a wake-up call."

"But if you lose your bet with Aunt Hilda, you'll be on kibble and water for another month," Sabrina said, ignoring the phone.

The cat chuckled. "I'm not going to lose. I took a cue from you and set the scale *back* half a pound."

"This is a WAKE-UP CALL!" The amplified voice jolted Sabrina and made Salem cringe.

Sabrina held up the offensive phone and shook it. "Stop it!"

"An interesting approach, but it's not going to work," Salem said.

"I know, but it makes me feel better." Sabrina stuffed the phone in her bag and covered her ears. That didn't work, either. "There's got to be some way to stop it from ringing back with this same stupid message."

"Whatever you did today, it must have been really bad," Salem said.

"The only not nice thing I've done today was when I changed the settings on the scale." Sabrina eyed the cat pointedly. "And *that* was justified."

"Perhaps, but the phone obviously didn't think so." Salem jumped to the table and licked the last speck of fish oil from the anchovy tin. "That's why it gave you a wake-up call."

"Wait a minute!" Sabrina sat bolt upright. "You mean wake-up call like in 'change your ways before it's too late' wake-up call? I thought it was an alarm!"

"It is." Salem hooked a claw on a pretzel. "It sounds the alarm when you've done something wrong so you can fix it—before whatever havoc you've created gets so bad it *can't* be fixed."

Sabrina was aghast. "I just wanted a cell phone—not a conscience!"

"Forgot to read the fine print again, didn't you?"

"Nobody likes a smart-aleck cat, you know."

Folding her arms, Sabrina pouted for a moment, then turned to Salem for clarification. "So it called me this morning because of the April Fools' joke I played on you?"

"That's my best guess." Salem tossed the pretzel in the air, opened his mouth, and caught it on a fang. "Neat trick, huh? Think it can get me a spot on *Real Pets*? I just love that show." He flipped the pretzel into his mouth with his tongue and crunched.

Sabrina wasn't listening. She was thinking back over the events of the morning. "The phone started ringing right after I got to school and stopped ringing after I apologized to you and reset the scale."

Salem wiped pretzel salt off his mouth. "Hardly enough considering *my* miserable morning, but apparently it satisfied the phone."

Sabrina nodded absently and reached for a pretzel. The prank she had played on Salem was pretty mean, especially after he had spent two weeks eating kibble to win his bet with Aunt Hilda. *I probably did deserve a wake-up call for that dirty trick, but there is a bright side!*

"So I just have to be nice to people—"

"And cats," Salem interjected.

"—and the phone will just be a phone and not the do-gooder police?"

"THIS IS A WAKE-UP CALL!"

Sabrina threw up her hands. "Now what?"

"All that ringing must have scrambled your

brain," Salem muttered, rolling his eyes. "What else have you done wrong today?"

"Nothing," Sabrina answered quickly, then wrinkled her nose. "Much. I just hurt my boyfriend's best friend's feelings, tried to cheat on a science report, intimidated two poor freshmen, evacuated the school, and got suspended."

"Is that all?" Salem asked.

"I'm out of here." Sabrina scooped her books off the floor and popped back into the school rest room.

Zelda closed out the shop's account file and turned off the laptop with a weary sigh. The financial situation was worse than she realized.

The Clock Shop had never turned a large profit, but until recently they had always brought in enough to pay the business expenses with something left over. Zelda had not been wildly enthusiastic when Hilda had given up the violin to sell clocks. It was only with reservations that Zelda had agreed to become a partner in the enterprise. One of her conditions had been that if the business went broke, they wouldn't dip into their other investments to bail it out.

"Cheer up! I brought lunch." Hilda pushed through the front door carrying two iced teas and sandwiches from the deli down the street.

"Did you hand out all those flyers?" Zelda made room on the counter.

"All one hundred. I covered at least five blocks in every direction except up and down. Hilda dragged two folding chairs out of the back room. "Has anyone come in?"

Zelda shook her head and sipped her tea. She wasn't looking forward to breaking the bad news to her volatile sister. Hilda didn't handle disappointment well.

"I'm sure the flyers will help. You'll see." Hilda unwrapped her sandwich.

"I hope so. I've become very fond of this old shop." Zelda sighed, her gaze sweeping the antique stands and display cases that held hundreds of clocks in all sizes, shapes, styles, and colors. Every single one was set to the exact same time. "I'll miss hearing all our clocks ticking off the seconds and bonging every hour on the hour."

"Are you going somewhere?" Hilda asked.

"No, but if business doesn't pick up soon, we'll have to close down." Anticipating Hilda's protest, Zelda added, "We had a deal, remember? The store has to pay for itself or we sell."

"No! I love the Clock Shop!" Hilda's eyes narrowed as she leaned toward Zelda. "Don't even think about selling, Zelda, or you'll be very sorry."

"Is that a threat?"

Hilda's mouth tightened in a smug smile. "Remember your tenth birthday?"

"You wouldn't dare!" Zelda had almost, but not quite, forgiven Hilda for ruining what should have been one of the happiest days of her life. Annoyed because Zelda could use magic to get *anything* she wanted for the whole day, a tenth birthday tradition, Hilda had cast a spell that turned anything Zelda wanted into a creepy crawly thing. Zelda's white pony had turned into a tortoise, and everything she had tried to eat had sprouted legs.

"Try me." Hilda lifted her chin in defiance.

"You gave your word, Hilda," Zelda reminded her. "Witch's honor."

"No, I didn't."

"Yes, you did," Zelda insisted, losing patience.

"I did?" Uncertainty replaced Hilda's stubborn determination.

"I'm positive." No matter how much Hilda loved the Clock Shop, Zelda knew she wouldn't break her witch's oath of honor. The consequences were much too dismal. "And you'll keep your word . . . unless you *want* to spend the next twenty-five years filling in craters on the moon."

"Not for all the clock shops in Massachusetts." Hilda tore the tops off three sugar packets and dumped them into her iced tea. "Which is why the lunar pothole project will *never* get done."

"I think that was the general idea," Zelda said. "Filling in the craters would kill the tourist trade." Zelda picked up her sandwich and put it down again. She couldn't eat when she was depressed.

"Don't we have some bonds that are maturing soon?" Hilda asked hopefully. "Or stocks we could cash in?"

"Yes, but that money goes into Sabrina's college

fund," Zelda said. "I don't want to lose the Clock Shop any more than you do, Hilda, but it would be irresponsible to risk Sabrina's future to save it. And I'm afraid there's no leeway in the household budget right now, either."

"Petty cash?" Hilda crossed her fingers.

"Five dollars and forty-seven cents."

"Cool! Let's go buy a lottery ticket!" Hilda held out her hand.

"No, there's got to be a better way." Zelda stood up, her jaw set with resolve. "Since when have we given up without a fight?"

"Never, but we've always been able to use magic." Hilda held up her finger.

"Hilda! Put that away! You know we can't use magic for personal gain."

Hilda quickly tucked her hands under her armpits. "If I ever meet the witch who made up that rule, I'll—"

Zelda looked toward the door, following Hilda's gaze, when she suddenly stopped talking. An elderly man holding a piece of paper paused in front of the window.

"Don't leave!" Hilda chewed her knuckle when the old man started to walk away. He halted abruptly and turned back.

"Looks like we've got a live one!" Zelda stashed the iced teas and sandwiches on the shelf under the counter.

Wearing a baggy suit and a brimmed hat, with a cane dangling from his arm, the old man pushed open the door and staggered inside. "I have to buy a clock. Now."

"Of course, sir." Zelda smiled. "What kind of clock are you looking for?"

"I don't care." The white-haired gentleman looked somewhat dazed as he lifted a travel clock off the nearest shelf, then glanced at the paper in his hand. "Is this one okay?"

"An excellent choice, sir. The batteries last for two years." Hilda walked around the counter.

"How much?" The man set the travel clock on the counter and pulled out his wallet.

"Thirty-two fifty with tax!" Zelda rang up the sale.

The man dropped two twenties on the counter. "Can I go now?"

"Is that one of our flyers?" Hilda asked.

The man shoved the flyer into Hilda's hand, pocketed his change, picked up his clock, and shuffled out the door.

"Wait!" Hilda grabbed a thirteen-hour watch from the basket by the door and ran outside. "Hey, mister! You forgot your wacky-witch-watch!"

The old man walked faster without looking back.

"That was a little strange, wasn't it?" Zelda stepped into the doorway.

Hilda nodded. "Now that you mention it, he did act like he had to buy a clock or else."

"Hey, lady!" a gruff voice barked.

"Who said that?" Startled, Hilda looked behind her.

Zelda yanked the flyer out of Hilda's hand and

held it up. A three-dimensional face appeared on the picture of the alarm clock.

"Go buy a clock!" the animated picture snapped. "Now!"

"Hilda!" Zelda gasped. "This is a *magical* flyer! What are we going to do?"

Hilda scowled. "Well, for starters that flyer needs to tone down its sales pitch."

Chapter 7

Sabrina hurried through the empty halls, hoping she didn't run into Mr. Kraft. Suspended students were expected to leave school immediately. *And I did,* she told herself. She just didn't want to explain coming back to take care of unfinished business. Besides, with luck she could talk the principal into unsuspending her before the school day ended.

Since she wasn't going to class, Sabrina ditched her books in her locker. She wished she could ditch the phone, too, but there was no point. It would just keep coming back like iron filings attracted to a magnet.

"This is a WAKE-UP CALL!"

"I'm working on it!" Sabrina opened her bag and berated the obnoxious cell phone through clenched teeth. "How am I supposed to put things right with people when *you* won't stop nagging me?"

Good question, Sabrina thought. She didn't dare

turn the Silver Cloud SDE off, because another accidental fire drill would get her expelled. *But maybe I can adjust the volume!*

Sabrina started to point, then stopped herself. She had a better success record for casting spells than Dreama, by about a hundred to one, but she decided not to risk another muting spell. Solving the problem would require something more mundane than magical.

> *Magic phone that's good for nothing,*
> *have a bag of cotton stuffing.*

Sabrina pointed, then grinned when clumps of billowy cotton instantly appeared in her bag.

"This is a wake-up call." The muffled phone voice was no louder than a harsh whisper.

"Just in time, too," Sabrina muttered when the bell rang. Slinging her bag over her shoulder, she ran to catch Brad and Harvey between classes.

On her way to Harvey's locker, Sabrina saw the two girls that she had driven out of the rest room. Anxious to make up for the wrongs she had done so her life could get back to normal, she dashed toward them.

The shorter girl saw Sabrina first. She grabbed her taller, blond friend and pointed. Both girls did an about-face and bolted down the hall in the opposite direction.

"Hey!" Sabrina couldn't let the opportunity pass. She had no idea who they were or when she would run into them again. Casting a quick point to stop their escape, she sprinted to catch up.

The younger girls seemed unaware that they were jogging in place without gaining ground until Sabrina planted herself in front of them. Sabrina flicked off another point to remove the spell, when they stopped moving to look down at their feet.

"Hi! We have to talk. I mean, I have to talk," Sabrina said with a sparkling smile. "About what happened earlier in the rest room."

Both girls just stared at her.

Will the phone give me credit for an apology if they don't accept it?

"Look, I shouldn't have snapped at you just because I have a wigged-out cell phone that's driving me crazy. How could you know I wasn't answering it on purpose?"

The girls looked at each other, obviously puzzled.

"Anyway, I'm really sorry. I should be ashamed of myself. I *am* ashamed of myself." Sabrina looked from one stricken face to the other. "Okay?"

The shorter girl frowned. "Stuff it!"

"I did! See?" Sabrina held up her bag full of cotton as the two girls pushed past her.

"This is a wake-up call."

Sabrina could barely hear the phone's repeating message. Convinced the decibel level had dropped, she continued down the hall. Harvey was throwing books, athletic equipment, and litter into his locker when she arrived.

"Hey, Sabrina!" Harvey caught a baseball that

rolled out of his stored junk pile. "Did you get your problem taken care of?"

"Well, not quite. That's why I have to talk to you." Sabrina noted that Harvey didn't seem angry that she had left the cafeteria so quickly. She leaned to the side and smiled at Brad, who was hovering behind Harvey. "You, too, Brad."

"Yeah?" Brad looked like he could care less whether she ever talked to him again. He shifted his books from one arm to the other, then glanced at her bag and frowned. "Your bag is talking."

"Cell phone." Sabrina struggled for an explanation. At least no one could hear *what* the phone was saying. "It's, uh—stuck in one of those automatic menus that go on forever."

"We'd better talk and walk at the same time or we'll be late." Harvey closed his locker and leaned on the door until the latch caught.

"Sure." Falling into step between the two boys, Sabrina launched into another hurried apology. "I know it sounded like I didn't want you to go to the game with Harvey and me Friday night, Brad, because I didn't."

Both boys stopped dead.

That was a totally foot-in-mouth moment. Sabrina paused with a sinking feeling. *But it was also the truth!* She hadn't intended to be that bluntly honest. It had just slipped out, but she suddenly realized that she couldn't lie her way out of the mess with Brad because lying was wrong. *Well, that's just great. Now I have to apologize* and *confess.*

"So far I'm not enjoying this conversation," Harvey said.

"Neither am I. I'll start over." Sabrina took a deep breath. "How's this? I was being completely selfish and unfair to you and Brad. It's the second biggest basketball game of the year, right?" She looked at Brad. "You don't really want to miss it, right?"

When Brad didn't respond, Sabrina cast a helpless glance at Harvey. "The more the merrier, right?"

"I always thought so," Harvey said.

"Me, too! I just forgot." Sabrina laughed nervously, then fixed Brad with pleading eyes. "So you'll change your mind about staying home and go with us, right?"

Brad shrugged. "I'll think about it."

"Great! You and Harvey can work out the details." Relieved to have that over with, Sabrina rushed away before she said something else she'd regret. She ducked into an empty classroom and pulled the Silver Cloud SDE out of her bag.

"This is a wake-up call." The tone had settled into its original monotone.

"Not perfect, but I must be making progress." As Sabrina started to leave to find Gordy, Mr. Wenzel, her science teacher, walked in.

"Sabrina?" Mr. Wenzel looked surprised to see her. "You're a little early for eighth period."

"Actually, I won't be here eighth period because Mr. Kraft suspended me for, uh—noise pollution." Sabrina winced, but the phone didn't start yelling. Apparently, a shaded truth was okay.

"I see." The teacher placed his planner on his desk and perched on the edge. "I'm sorry to hear that, but I'm glad you stopped by to hand in your report."

"Actually, my report isn't done. In fact, I tried to borrow Gordy's report to use as a reference because I couldn't go to the library, but he wouldn't give it to me. I was only going to cheat a little." Sabrina tried to look contrite. "And that's probably more than you needed to know."

Mr. Wenzel heaved a disappointed sigh. "Suspended and an F for your science report. You're not having a very good day, are you?"

"Believe it or not, I've had worse." Sabrina excused herself and left before she felt compelled to explain that aging decades in a week or turning green with envy were a lot more traumatic than owning a phone that doubled as an ethics monitor. On her way to Mr. Kraft's office, she pulled the phone out of her bag to check its status.

"This is a wake-up call. This is a wake-up call. This is—"

With a weary sigh, Sabrina buried the phone in the cotton muffler again. As near as she could figure, Mr. Kraft was the last person on her list of wrongs to right.

The school secretary wasn't behind the counter in the outer office. Sabrina didn't want to delay and gently rapped on Mr. Kraft's door. When she heard a grunt, she assumed the cranky principal had given permission to enter and stepped inside.

Mr. Kraft was asleep in his chair with his head thrown back and his mouth open, snoring.

Sabrina wasn't sure what to do. She had to talk him into letting her back into school, but if she woke him up, she might just make him angrier. A fly landed on his nose, solving the problem.

"Huh? What?" Mr. Kraft jerked awake. The fly flew off his face as he quickly composed himself. When he realized Sabrina was standing by the door, he flinched. "How long have you been here?"

"Just a few seconds. I knocked."

"Isn't it customary to wait for someone to say come in?" Mr. Kraft adjusted his glasses and averted his gaze to fiddle with some papers on his desk.

"I thought you did, but I guess I just heard you snoring and thought—"

"I do *not* snore!" Mr. Kraft nervously straightened his tie and smoothed back his hair. He looked at her narrowly. "Were you sent here to spy on me?"

Sabrina blinked. "By whom for what?"

"Never mind." The principal hesitated, looking past her for a thoughtful moment. He snapped back with a slight shake of his head. "Didn't I suspend you?"

"Yes, that's why I'm here." Sabrina moved closer to his desk. "I didn't deliberately evacuate the school, Mr. Kraft. The big noise wasn't my fault. Well, not exactly. More like indirectly."

"Trying to confuse me won't work. Explain or get out." Mr. Kraft picked up a pen and opened a folder. "Not that it will do you any good."

Sabrina wasn't sure *how* to explain. Mr. Kraft

60

would never believe the truth, but she had to be honest to shut down the cell phone.

Mr. Kraft's gaze shifted to Sabrina's bag. "Do you have a tape recorder in that bag?"

"No! It's this stupid phone!" Sabrina pulled out the Silver Cloud SDE.

"This is a wake-up call."

Mr. Kraft's temper flared. "I do not appreciate the joke, Ms. Spellman. If the school board has a problem with how I'm doing my job—"

"Believe me, Mr. Kraft, this is no joke." Sabrina jammed the phone back into her bag. "It started out as a joke when Salem told me my aunts were getting me a cell phone and then I found out they weren't. There's nothing more annoying than a cat with a warped sense of humor who likes April Fools'."

"Do tell?" Mr. Kraft settled back and rubbed his temples.

Hoping the phone wouldn't hold her responsible for his headache, too, Sabrina continued. "So I got this phone from the Other Realm for a free one-week trial, but the sales elf didn't tell me it was an electronic character cop." She huffed in disgust. "You just can't trust anybody these days."

"Sad, but true." Mr. Kraft sighed.

"So now it won't shut up until I fix everything I messed up today, which is why it was blaring like a fire alarm in the rest room, only I didn't know that was the reason at the time." Desperate, Sabrina leaned forward and clasped her hands to beg. "So you just have to let me back into school, Mr. Kraft, and please don't tell my aunts you kicked me out!"

"That is the most ridiculous story I've ever heard," Mr. Kraft said after a long pause.

"It's the only one I've got." Sabrina held her breath.

"All right." Mr. Kraft raised his hands in surrender. "You're not suspended, but only because I can retell that completely illogical excuse in the teachers' lounge."

"Thank you!" Sabrina turned to leave. "Is it okay if I get unsuspended as of tomorrow morning? I already got an F in science."

"You Spellmans *like* to live dangerously, don't you?"

"Gotta go." Sabrina raced into the outer office and pulled the phone out again. It was silent. "Woo hoo!"

"Quiet!" The school secretary walked in with a cup of coffee. "This is a school!"

"Sorry." Clutching the phone to her chest, Sabrina headed for the hall. The phone rang just as she reached the door. Since all her misdeeds had been cleared up, she answered without hesitation. "Hello?"

"This is a wake-up call."

"What?" Sabrina shrieked. "There must be some mistake!"

"Shhhh!" the secretary admonished her again.

"This is a wake-up call," the phone insisted.

Sabrina cupped her hand around her mouth and the phone. "But I haven't done anything wrong in the past two minutes!"

"This is a wake-up call."

Frantic, Sabrina muffled the phone with her hand and thought back over her meeting with Mr. Kraft. She hadn't lied about the phone's Klaxon ring or tried to put the blame on Dreama. And Mr. Kraft had lifted her suspension. So what terrible wrong could the phone possibly want her to set right?

"Mr. Kraft is the one who was goofing off with a midafternoon nap." Sabrina stiffened as a possible explanation for the latest wake-up call flashed through her mind. It wanted her to report the truth! Sabrina hesitated, but it was her only choice. She moved back into the office. "Excuse me."

"Yes?" The secretary looked up.

The phone rang.

Sabrina ignored it. "Someone should probably know that Mr. Kraft fell asleep on the job."

The phone did not ring again.

Chapter 8

Hilda paced in the back room of the Clock Shop while she waited for a reply from Duplicates Done. It had been five minutes since she had sent her note to the company asking for a refund on the flyers. She had plenty of barter magic in her account and wouldn't miss a pinch of spell, but Zelda had been adamant. *Too bad, too,* Hilda thought. The travel clock the old man had bought had been their only sale in the past three days.

"And he didn't even take a witch-watch, so we saved an extra thirty dollars!" Hilda frowned, realizing that that rationale lacked a certain logic. If she hadn't bought the thirteen-hour watches in the first place, the Clock Shop wouldn't be another thousand dollars closer to bankruptcy.

"We are *not* selling the Clock Shop!" Frustrated, Hilda whacked the toaster, which was actually a postal portal between the Other Realm and the mortal world. "What is taking so long?"

The toaster dinged and popped up a letter.

"Finally." Hilda absently tore open the envelope. One way or another, she was determined to save the Clock Shop without going back on her witch's word of honor. Their investments covered the Spellman family's financial needs, but losing the business would be a blow to her pride.

I'd rather shovel dirt on the moon than spend the next six months listening to Zelda say I told you so, Hilda thought as she scanned the memo from Duplicates Done. A slow smile brightened her face when she realized all was not lost. With a little creative justification, she could turn the bad news into an advantage.

Pocketing the paper, Hilda dashed through the door into the store and froze. When she had gone into the back a few minutes ago, Zelda had been dusting the shelves to keep busy. Now there were five customers demanding her harried sister's attention.

"What happened?" Hilda stepped behind the counter.

"*This* happened!" Zelda shoved a flyer into Hilda's hand, then turned back to a well-dressed woman who was waiting with her credit card in hand.

When Hilda looked at the flyer, the clock face was automatically activated. Instead of an intimidating bark, this flyer spoke with a cultured arrogance. "The Seth Thomas mantel clock is a steal at two hundred and twenty-five dollars."

"She's buying the Seth Thomas?" Hilda whispered in Zelda's ear. The antique clock had been in the inventory when she had bought the business. They had given up trying to sell it months ago.

"She is if you'll leave me alone to wait on her," Zelda hissed. Smiling as she turned back to the customer, Zelda ran the woman's credit card through the authorization machine and handed her the slip to sign.

"How much is this one?" A construction worker, chewing gum and wearing a hard hat, palmed a delicate clock set in Waterford crystal.

"A hundred and fifty." Hilda flinched when he tossed the fragile clock in the air and caught it. "Wouldn't you like something a little more . . . hefty?"

"Naw." The big man grinned. "My sister's getting married and she loves this prissy stuff. I'll take it."

"Great! I'll gift-wrap it." Hilda grabbed the clock as he was about to shove it in his pocket. She didn't want a hassle if he broke the clock *before* he paid. "No extra charge!"

"This is free, too, right?" The man looked at the wacky-witch-watch he had already strapped on his wrist. "My old one broke, and I hate not knowing what time it is."

"That's a thirteen-hour watch," Hilda said as she placed the Waterford clock into a tissue-lined box.

"Yeah. I can use a couple extra hours a day. I never have enough time." He laughed and playfully punched her arm. "That was a joke."

"Right." Hilda completed the sale and picked up

the flyer the man dropped on his way out. "What was your come-on line?" Hilda asked the flyer.

"Yo! You gotta go get one of them free witch-watches, man!" The clock face on the flyer winked and made a thumbs-up gesture with its minute hand.

"Whatever works." Hilda put the used flyer in a cardboard file box Zelda had set behind the counter.

"How much did your guy spend?" the new flyer asked the old man's flyer.

"Thirty bucks, but he was a charity case." The bully flyer huffed. "So back off, buster!"

"Pipe down or I'll rip both of you in half!" Hilda put the lid on the file box.

Zelda finished sealing a deal with a teenaged boy who had purchased a space-age-style clock that played the opening bars of a different science fiction movie theme every hour. She took the boy's flyer and spun around to face Hilda. "What did Duplicates Done say? Are they going to give us our magic back?"

"Afraid not. Special order, no returns." Hilda beamed. "Isn't that great?"

"No! It's a disaster!" Zelda lowered her voice when the three people who were still browsing cast curious glances her way. "These are *magic* flyers!"

"You noticed?" Hilda rolled her eyes. Since she had not specified any preferences, Duplicates Done had conjured the flyers with the standard power-of-suggestion feature just as it would have for an Other Realm business. Mortals wouldn't remember that their flyers had actually spoken to them, only that they really needed to buy clocks. "Chill, Zelda! The tailored-to-the-individual marketing add-on was free."

"Does this one come in blue?" A young woman held up a red kitchen wall clock shaped like an apple with a green stem and leaves.

"Do they have blue apples where you come from?" Hilda asked.

"You *really* like red," the woman's flyer said.

"I'll be with you in a moment, dear." Zelda smiled at the customer, then drew Hilda into a conference huddle. "We can't use these flyers to sell our clocks, Hilda."

"It's okay, Zelda. The customers forget all about the flyers as soon as they buy something."

"Even so," Zelda pressed, "there are *always* dire consequences when magic is used for personal gain."

"And there are exceptions to every rule," Hilda said. "We've got a loophole. *I* didn't order magic flyers. It's not our fault Duplicates Done assumed that's what we wanted."

"So?"

"So it's not like we're using magic on purpose," Hilda explained. "We can't get the flyers back, either—not until the customers *bring* them back."

"Oh, I hadn't thought of that." Zelda paused with a worried frown. "Still, I'm not sure that defense will satisfy the Witches' Council."

"What the Witches' Council doesn't know won't hurt us." Hilda waved at a middle-aged couple as they entered the shop. "I handed out a hundred flyers, Zelda. If they all do their job, we won't have to sell the Clock Shop!"

"But we might need to hire some extra help," Zelda said when six more people came in.

"You take the register." Fixing a fake smile on her face, Hilda ran to stop a harried mother's toddler from climbing the grandfather clock in the front corner.

Sabrina trudged along the sidewalks of Westbridge lost in fretful thought. She had not been able to find Salem when she had gone home to change into jeans and a long-sleeved T-shirt for work. She had questions about the wake-up call she had gotten in the school office, but the cat was not taking up space on her bed as usual. He had probably curled up to sleep off his feast in one of his many hiding places where he wouldn't be disturbed.

"A lot of good that does me," Sabrina mumbled as she opened the coffeehouse door. "There's never an ex-warlock cat around when you really need a consultant!"

"Anything I can do to help?" Josh finished watering the ivy hanging in the window and smiled over his shoulder. "I know a lot about a lot of stuff."

"Uh, well—" Sabrina faltered. Josh had become a good friend since she had started working at the coffeehouse. She couldn't lie to him without setting off the phone, but she didn't want to reject his help and hurt his feelings, either. She was pretty sure Josh had a crush on her. The only thing that kept him from asking her out was Harvey and a few years' difference in their ages. There was only so much rejection a guy could take.

"Don't tell me you and Harvey had a fight?" Josh almost smiled, but he remembered to look concerned at the last second.

Sabrina hesitated again. Harvey hadn't been too happy when she had confessed she didn't want Brad to join them at the play-off game, but they hadn't argued. "No fight," she answered honestly. "Do you know anything about cell phones with a one-track mind?"

Josh's face clouded. "If you don't want to talk about your problems with me, Sabrina, just say so. Don't"—a sudden smile replaced his defensive mode—"oh, I get it. You're putting me on because it's April Fools' Day."

"It definitely has something to do with April Fools' Day." Sabrina started toward the storeroom to get her apron.

"Catch the rest rooms first, okay?"

Sabrina glanced back. "April Fools'?"

"No. For real." Josh waved her away and moved the watering can to the philodendron.

Sabrina caught herself before she pointed to throw off his aim so he would drench his shoes. There was no way the Witch Wireless phone in her back pocket would let her get away with a magical act of petty revenge. "But I can't believe I'm the only employee in this place who knows how to clean a bathroom."

Business was slow, which wasn't unusual for a

Monday afternoon. After Sabrina finished the rest rooms, she took out the trash, refilled the condiments, stocked the shelves with extra napkins and boxes of straws, and waited on a few customers. Josh was in a good mood, and the first hour flew by without incident, but not without struggle and stress.

Sabrina had never realized how often she did little things that might qualify as "wrong." She was so worried about triggering another wake-up call that she was conscious of every word and action.

"Miss!" A pretty college girl wearing an Emerson sweatshirt waved a spoon. "This is dirty!"

"One clean spoon coming right up!" Sabrina finished wiping down her table and lugged a bus tub full of dirty cups and plates to the sink. The spoon container was empty. "What? No clean spoons?"

"I haven't washed them yet." Josh pulled a dirty spoon from the machine and handed it to her. "The owner wants to save on the electric bill so I can't run the washer until it's full."

"This has junk on it." Sabrina held the grimy spoon at arm's length and grimaced with disgust.

"Clean it." Shaking his head, Josh carried sandwiches to a table by the front door.

"What's taking forever?" The Emerson girl shot Sabrina an annoyed glance. "I'd like to stir in my sugar and drink this coffee before it gets cold."

The attractive, dark-haired girl sitting across from her almost choked trying not to laugh.

Don't you know that sarcasm breeds contempt,

Sabrina thought as she wiped the gunk off the spoon with a dirty towel, *and bunches of bugs in your next cup of Café Mocha Supreme.* She took a step toward the table, then quickly backtracked to wash the spoon with soap and water. The Silver Cloud SDE probably wouldn't tolerate spreading germs via dirty silverware, either.

Stir this! Sabrina considered turning the sugar on the girl's table into sand. Having to apologize would almost be worth watching the disagreeable college student pick grit out of her gleaming, perfect teeth.

Almost, but why go looking for trouble? Sabrina delivered the clean spoon and kept her impulse to point under control and her unkind thoughts to herself.

"We need more napkins." The girl held up the napkin holder without looking at Sabrina.

"Sure." Sabrina refilled the holder, dashed back to the table, and set it down gently. In her mind she imagined changing the napkins into white bats. She smiled as she visualized the creatures in frenzied flight around the girl's head. "Can I get you anything else?"

"Yeah. You can get lost and leave us alone."

Sabrina glared, her finger twitching at her side.

The cell phone rang.

Josh looked up and frowned.

Sabrina whipped the phone out of her pocket and darted into the corner. When she answered, the phone repeated its all too familiar message. "You can read my thoughts, too? I can't control what I think!"

"This is a wake-up call."

"Right. Got it." Disconnecting, Sabrina hurried back to the table. Both girls wrinkled their noses as though she was wearing Stench Of Sewer perfume. "Look, I know this won't make any sense, but I apologize for thinking about all the rotten things I'd like to do to you. Bugs in your coffee, bats in your hair—"

The cell phone rang again.

"Sabrina!" Josh motioned her to come.

"In a minute!" Flustered, Sabrina turned her back on the girls to answer the phone. She had confessed and apologized, and she hadn't had a bad thought in the past ten seconds!

"This is a wake-up call."

Sabrina stabbed the Off button, her mind reeling. Maybe the phone *didn't* know what she was thinking. Maybe it was calling for the same reason it had called when she'd left Mr. Kraft's office. *Because someone* else *did something wrong and I'm supposed to do something about it!*

Sabrina spun to face the girls.

The Emerson girl sneered with disdain. "It's beyond me why Josh would hire a loser like you."

"Well, I've got news for you." Sabrina swallowed hard. She wouldn't know if her theory was correct unless she tested it. "Being weird is better than being rude and obnoxious like you. If you don't change your attitude, you'll have a lonely, miserable life with no friends."

Both girls burst out laughing.

"Now, Sabrina!" Josh called.

"Excuse me." Sabrina hurried back to the counter.

"Got yourself a cell phone, huh?" Josh arched an eyebrow.

"Yeah, and it isn't ringing!" Sabrina's nervous laugh died in her throat. *Which means my theory is right and I've just been deputized by the do-gooder police!*

"Cool, but why don't you put it in the storeroom while you're working."

"I can't! I mean, I just got it today and—wait! Why don't I just turn it off?" She held the phone up and went through the motions of hitting the Off button again. "There."

Josh hesitated, rubbing the back of his neck and exhaling. "Okay, but if it rings again—"

"It won't. I'm totally on good behavior from now on." Noting Josh's baffled expression, Sabrina jumped to the coffee counter to distract him. As she began measuring coffee into filters to save time during the dinner hour rush, the two Emerson girls came up to the counter to pay.

"How you doing, Evelyn?" Josh asked pleasantly.

"Terrible." The girl sighed. "The service was lousy and my Café Mocha Supreme was made with burned coffee. The whipped cream was a little off, too. Very bad for business, don't you think?"

"I'll take care of it," Josh said evenly. "No charge—"

Uh-oh! Sabrina grabbed the Silver Cloud SDE from her pocket just as it started to ring and hit

Send to silence the sound. She didn't have to answer to know why the phone was calling, and if she didn't act quickly, it would just ring back.

"She's lying, Josh!" Sabrina blurted out the accusation as she turned.

"Sabrina!" Josh snapped, his gaze narrowing with warning. "The customer is *always* right, remember?"

"Except when the customer is wrong," Sabrina countered. "Her Café Mocha Supreme was made with *fresh* coffee. She watched me brew it!"

"I don't have to take insults from the hired help!" Fuming, Evelyn lashed out at Josh. "Deal with this problem before I come back."

Sabrina huffed as Evelyn and her friend stormed out. "She's got some nerve."

"True, but then she's the owner's daughter." Josh sighed. "And you're fired."

Chapter 9

Sabrina was still in shock when she walked in the front door of her aunts' Victorian house. Being suspended, getting an F in science, and upsetting Harvey all seemed trivial compared to getting fired! How could Josh side with Evelyn the Contemptible Coed against her?

"Because *she's* the boss's daughter and *he* can't afford to be unemployed, either." Sabrina slammed the door closed. "At least he doesn't have a cell phone running his life."

"Having a bad day?" Salem was lounging on the library table behind the couch.

"It ranks somewhere between mucking out the bat cave at witch camp and running barefoot through the Sahara at high noon." Sabrina glowered at the cat. If Salem hadn't zinged her with his April Fools' prank, she wouldn't have decided she *had* to have a cell phone today. However, blaming him wouldn't solve the problem, and it might start another round of wake-up calls.

"That bad, huh?" Hilda's head popped into view at one end of the couch.

"We ran ourselves ragged all day, too." Zelda peeked over the top of the sofa at the other end. "But we put money in the bank instead of taking it out for a change."

"Does that mean I don't have to pay my long-distance bill?" Sabrina asked. Now that she didn't work at the coffeehouse, she had no hope of paying it off.

"No, but you can pull up a chair and join us. We're celebrating with pizza and the Tarzan Film Festival on the Jungle Channel." Hilda waved the remote.

"Pizza sounds good, but I think I'll pass on Tarzan." As Sabrina walked by, she kept her back turned away from her aunts so they wouldn't see the cell phone in her hip pocket. She flopped in the armchair with a weary sigh. "I'm not in the mood for watching a hunk in a breechcloth yodel and swing on vines. It might cheer me up."

"In that case," Salem said, "let's watch that sci-fi classic *Plan Nine From Outer Space.*"

Sprawled on her end of the sofa with her feet propped on the coffee table, Hilda craned her neck to look at the cat. "Which is considered by many to be the worst movie ever made, including me."

"Which is why *I* need my own TV set complete with satellite service," Salem shot back. "Then we can avoid these family arguments."

"Who's arguing?" Hilda fluffed the large throw pillow behind her and leaned back. "We're watching *Tarzan*."

"Was the coffeehouse busy, too, Sabrina?" Zelda sat up and stretched.

"No, it was pretty slow."

"Is that why Josh let you go early?" Hilda aimed the remote and turned on the TV. The credits of an old black-and-white film were rolling, and she muted the sound.

"Well, he let me go and it was early." Sabrina tensed, but the Silver Cloud SDE didn't ring. Apparently, it didn't understand that some phrases had double meanings. *Lucky for me.*

However, her aunts were on the verge of asking questions Sabrina didn't want to answer, especially since she had to tell the truth. They'd find out she had lost her job eventually, but now was not the time. She couldn't explain why Josh had fired her without telling them she had signed away control of her life for a Witch Wireless cell phone. An immediate diversion was imperative.

Sabrina stood up. "Anyone want something to drink while I'm in the kitchen?"

"Club soda and lime," Hilda said.

"Make that two." Zelda held up two fingers. "Too bad you have to work at the coffeehouse tomorrow. We could use you at the Clock Shop."

"Boy, could we!" Hilda rubbed her foot. "We sold thirty clocks today."

Salem's ears perked forward. "Giving away those

thirteen-hour watches Hilda got stuck with actually worked?"

"Sort of," Hilda said. "Only six people wanted them."

"So business is booming again?" Sabrina asked.

Zelda nodded. "For the moment. It's a bit too hectic for Hilda and me to handle by ourselves."

"Problem solved, Aunt Zelda. I'm not working at the coffeehouse tomorrow, so I can put in some time at the Clock Shop." Sabrina didn't mind helping out when she could, but she volunteered with reservations. She'd have to take the cell phone with her.

"We'll deduct your wages from the phone bill," Zelda said. "Is that okay with you?"

"Perfect." Sabrina started toward the kitchen, muttering under her breath. "Right now all I want is to be phone-problem free."

Everyone looked up when booming thunder from the upstairs linen closet rattled the pictures on the walls.

"Pizza's here!" Salem peered at the clock on the table. "Figures. One minute later and Presto Pizza would have picked up the tab."

"Would you mind, Sabrina?" Hilda rubbed her back. "I'm too sore to walk and too pooped to pop."

"Got it." Changing course, Sabrina dashed up the stairs and threw open the linen closet door. A short, fat, green goblin wearing a foam hat designed like a wedge of pepperoni pizza shoved two pizza boxes into her hands.

"Just charge it to Zelda Spellman's account." Sabrina started to close the door.

"Wait!" The delivery goblin blocked the door with a clawed foot. "Tell the guy who called in the order that we were all out of squid bits."

"That's the best news I've heard all day." Sabrina's stomach churned with disgust.

"So we substituted raw jellyfish globs." The goblin's red eyes glowed when it grinned, displaying two rows of needle-sharp, yellow teeth. "Where's my tip?"

"Is mortal money okay?"

"Why do you think I took this lousy route?" The green guy grunted. "Newt nuggets and batwing dust won't buy me a ringside seat at the next World Wrestling Smack Down."

Balancing the pizza boxes on one hand, Sabrina dug five dollars out of her pocket for him and ran back downstairs. Salem was sitting on the coffee table with a paper napkin tied around his neck.

"The one with the jellyfish globs is Salem's." Sabrina set the boxes down and glanced at her aunts. "Unless you two have developed a taste for disgusting, slimy stuff."

"Gag!" Hilda frowned. "Sabotaging the order in your favor again, huh, Salem?"

"I didn't order jellyfish!" Salem declared, incensed.

"They were out of squid bits," Sabrina explained. She cast a curious glance at the cat. "Are you sure you want to eat this before you weigh in?"

"He already did," Zelda said. "Right before you got home. He won the bet by four ounces."

"Hard to believe, but we've got the most accurate scale money can buy." Hilda shrugged.

The blood suddenly drained from Sabrina's face. "How many ounces in a pound?"

"Sixteen. Why?" Hilda placed the open jellyfish pizza box in front of the cat.

Sabrina did some quick mental computation. Eight ounces in half a pound plus one added up to nine ounces, the amount Salem had set back the scale. If the scale indicated he had lost two pounds and four ounces, then he had lost only *one* pound and *eleven* ounces. He had actually lost the bet by five ounces!

And now I know about it!

"He cheated," Sabrina said before the Silver Cloud SDE could ring with a wake-up call.

"What?" Salem yelped, his eyes widening.

"What?" Hilda and Zelda asked in unison. Hilda snatched the jellyfish pizza out from under Salem's nose.

"He changed the settings on the scale." Sabrina felt like a traitor, but it couldn't be helped. If she didn't rat out Salem now, the phone would nag her until she did. "I'm sorry, Salem, but fair's fair. Aunt Hilda won the bet."

Salem stared at her, his mouth hanging open in dumbfounded disbelief. He started to sputter a protest, but no sound came out.

"Salem, how could you?" Zelda shook her head and sighed with disappointment.

"Yeah! Now we've got a whole pizza nobody

else can eat!" Hilda pointed, and the box vanished.

Salem sank onto his stomach and buried his face in his paws. His pathetic sobbing was more than Sabrina could stand.

"I'm not hungry. Guilt and pizza are a really rotten combination."

Sabrina ran back upstairs and threw herself on her bed. She didn't know what to do, and she couldn't talk to anyone about the problem. Salem certainly wouldn't be anxious to help her now, and she couldn't tell her aunts about the phone. Asking Gwen for magical advice would be as futile as asking for Mr. Kraft's opinion about the latest alternative music CDs.

"But Gwen knows what it's like to totally mess up, so at least she'll be sympathetic." Sabrina sat up, automatically reached for the phone on her nightstand, then remembered her long-distance privileges had been cut off. Her new cell phone, however, had unlimited service. She felt better just dialing Gwen's number. After all she had been through that day, she was finally using the phone as a phone!

"Gwen! Guess what I'm calling you on!"

"A phone? No, wait." Gwen hesitated. "Is this a trick question, Sabrina?"

"Never mind. Just listen. I got this Witch Wireless one-week-free trial cell phone today. It's a Silver Cloud SDE and so small it fits in my pocket."

"Oh, that is so cool!" Gwen gushed.

"That was the general idea, but it's turned my life

into a serial disaster!" Sabrina quickly explained the problem. "I can't even leave it somewhere because it comes right back. The company must have programmed it to home in on my magical frequencies or something."

"Did the salesperson tell you that then?" Gwen asked.

"No." Sabrina sighed. "Nancy didn't explain exactly what the wake-up call feature does, either."

"Well, it seems to me that since Nancy misrepresented the product, you might be able to return it to Witch Wireless!"

Sabrina blinked. "Gwen, sometimes you are positively brilliant. Gotta go! Thanks." After hanging up, Sabrina checked the magic book for the Witch Wireless customer service number and dialed.

A computer voice similar to the phone's voice answered. "Please punch in your Witch Wireless number and hit the Caldron key."

Sabrina complied.

"Please wait while we access your account."

Sabrina drummed her fingers while she listened to the long list of options on the automatic menu.

"For returns, please press thirty-four."

"Finally." Sabrina touched the numerals three and four.

"Your Silver Cloud Super Deluxe Edition cannot be returned until your current contract expires next Monday at seven-forty-six A.M. eastern standard time, Mortal World. Good-bye."

"Wait! I want to talk to a real witch!"

The phone went dead.

Sabrina threw up her hands in exasperation. "No wonder they give these phones away free. It's the only way they can get rid of them!"

Too upset to sleep, Sabrina left the house hoping some fresh air would settle her jangled nerves. She started walking with no particular destination in mind, her thoughts in turmoil. The Silver Cloud SDE, which she had tucked back into her pocket, was like an anchor around her neck. Having to correct her own mistakes was a pain, but being forced to snitch on everyone else was worse. She could control her own actions, but her unsuspecting friends and family were at the mercy of the persistent phone with its insidious wake-up calls.

By the time Sabrina had walked through downtown Westbridge and was circling back along quieter, residential streets, the gnawing in her stomach was stronger than the guilt that had wiped out her appetite. She headed for a neighborhood mini-mall at the end of the block. A hot fudge sundae wouldn't help her out of her phone predicament, but it would satisfy her hunger.

Sabrina paused outside the door of the Super Scoop Ice Cream Emporium and dug several crumpled dollar bills out of her front pocket. She stared at the wad of money for a long moment. Now that she didn't work at the coffeehouse, she wouldn't have tips to use as a splurge fund after today. "Everyone who's standing on the brink of total ruin deserves a final fling."

The ice cream shop was empty except for the attendant behind the counter. He was scraping ice out of a freezer, and he turned when the bell rang as Sabrina opened the door.

Two pairs of eyes locked in a stunned gaze.

Sabrina broke the awkward silence. "Mr. Kraft?"

"What are you doing here?" Mr. Kraft snapped in his usual authoritative tone, but the effect was completely negated when his upside-down ice-cream cone hat fell forward to cover his eyes. The embarrassed principal, with rolled-up shirtsleeves and an apron splattered with forty-two flavors, pushed the comical hat back on to his head and crossed his arms.

"I wanted a hot fudge sundae." Sabrina held out her money.

"What flavor ice cream?" Mr. Kraft mumbled. He grabbed an ice cream scoop from a container.

"French vanilla." Sabrina warily approached the counter as Mr. Kraft picked up a paper cup and dug into the French vanilla container. "What are you doing here?"

"Scooping ice cream. What does it look like?"

"I meant *why* are you here?" Sabrina gasped. "Did you get fired, too?"

"No, I didn't get fired." Mr. Kraft slammed the cup full of ice cream on the counter and took the metal top off the hot fudge warmer. He ladled the gooey chocolate topping into the sundae cup with a vengeance. "I didn't get a raise or a bonus, either, and I can't afford a fishing boat with twin engines, a flying bridge, and all the latest electronic gear on my salary. Satisfied?"

Sabrina nodded and flinched when he shook the whipped cream can, then sprayed it all over the wall.

"Now see what you made me do?" Using both hands to aim, Mr. Kraft put a dab of whipped cream on Sabrina's sundae, sprinkled on a few nuts, and crowned it with a cherry. He set the cup on the counter and growled, "Anything else?"

"No, this is—fine." Sabrina took the sloppy sundae, paid, and lifted a plastic spoon from a holder on the shelf on her way out.

"Sabrina!" Mr. Kraft ran after her. Obviously self-conscious, he leaned against the doorjamb, wiped his hands on his apron, and cleared his throat. "I'd really appreciate it if you didn't tell anyone about this. If Mrs. Markum on the school board finds out—well, you know what she thinks about—ahem—moonlighting."

And this is a problem for you? Sabrina had to smile at the irony, but she said, "I totally understand, Mr. Kraft."

"Good, good." Nodding, Mr. Kraft stepped back and let the door swing closed.

As Sabrina walked away, she looked back to see Mr. Kraft rip the ice-cream-cone hat off his head, throw it on the floor, and jump up and down on it. "Boy, do I understand."

Sabrina was halfway down the block when the cell phone rang. She sighed. Setting her half-eaten sundae on a fence post, she dialed information and got the number she needed. Despising herself but having no choice, she punched in the numbers.

"Mrs. Markum? Mr. Kraft is sleeping on the job at Westbridge High because he's moonlighting at Super Scoop."

Chapter 10

Mr. Kraft was waiting in ambush at her locker when she arrived at school that morning.

"Read that!" Mr. Kraft shoved a letter at Sabrina.

Startled, Sabrina took the paper in a shaking hand. She had been so worried about saying, doing, or seeing something that would prompt a wake-up call that she hadn't seen the principal waiting by her locker. "What is it?"

"Official notification from Mrs. Markum." The furious man yanked the paper back and waved it in Sabrina's face. He was breathing so hard that he popped a button on his vest. "The school board is going to review my record before they renew my employment contract, and it's all your fault!"

"My fault?" Sabrina decided to bluff. She hadn't given Mrs. Markum her name, so Mr. Kraft couldn't be absolutely positive she had called the school board member last night.

"Nobody else knows I've been working at Super Scoop." Mr. Kraft leaned closer, driving his point home in Sabrina's face. "Not my mother, my ex-wife, my obnoxiously perfect brother, or your aunt Zelda. Nobody but *you*!"

The Silver Cloud SDE wouldn't let Sabrina lie, so she didn't say anything.

Squaring his shoulders, Mr. Kraft folded the letter and slipped it inside his jacket. "I can't prove you called Mrs. Markum, but I'll be watching you every minute of every day. One false move and you're out of here."

"Define 'out of here.' "

"Expelled. Finished. Out of Westbridge High." Mr. Kraft smiled as though he'd like nothing better than to get rid of her. "I don't care if you don't graduate. I don't care if you can't get into college. I don't care about anything except keeping my job and getting my boat. Understand?"

Sabrina nodded, numb.

Sabrina ducked into the rest room between second and third periods. Except for the confrontation with Mr. Kraft, she had managed to avoid bad behavior so far—hers and everyone else's. She was dismayed to see Maureen Brinks primping at the mirror, but the eccentric girl was a straight A student and so pleasant that Sabrina didn't anticipate any trouble.

I just won't mention the neon green hair, and everything will be fine. Sabrina stepped up beside the girl and smiled. "How's it going, Maureen?"

"Great!" When Maureen grinned, the rhinestone she had glued to a front tooth sparkled in the fluorescent light. So did the red sequined dragon on her sweatshirt and the glitter in her blue eye shadow. "How's it going with you?"

"Could be better." Sabrina was deliberately ambiguous to confuse the watchdog phone.

"Yeah. Me, too."

Sabrina just tightened her smile and nodded. Self-conscious about being eyed so strangely by other students, Maureen went out of her way to be agreeable so people would like her.

Maureen leaned over the sink and closed one eye. "Do you think the glitter eye shadow is too much?"

Sabrina's heart lurched. Evasion was the only safe route out of the truth trap the girl had inadvertently set. "You don't really want my opinion, Maureen. Who am I to say?"

Maureen opened her eye. "Only one of the coolest girls in school." Maureen began counting off the reasons why on her fingers. "You're gorgeous, fun, smart, nice, and you have a great boyfriend. So what do you think?" The girl turned toward Sabrina and blinked her eyes several times.

"Well, I—I think—" Sabrina just couldn't bring herself to hurt the girl's feelings. *Maybe the phone will take that into consideration!* "It looks totally cool, Maureen. Very—chic."

The phone rang.

Sabrina exhaled as she retrieved it from her bag, hit Send to answer, turned it off, and put it back.

"See? You have a cell phone!" Maureen's eyes widened. "And you're so cool you don't even *care* if you know who calls!"

Sabrina took a deep breath. She wasn't mystified about the wake-up call she had just gotten. The phone knew she wasn't doing Maureen any favors by not being honest. Agreeing with the phone's assessment didn't make her task any easier, though.

"There's something you should know, Maureen," Sabrina said, hoping to cushion the harsh words to follow. "You're a really terrific, fun person and everyone thinks so, but if you don't want to be listed in the yearbook as the class joke—and I know for a fact that the committee is thinking about it— you've got to make some changes."

Maureen's smile vanished.

Sabrina couldn't stop now that she had started. "The kaleidoscopic glitter look just doesn't work. If you lost the sparkles and let your hair go back to its natural color and toned down your wardrobe, you'd—"

Maureen burst into tears.

"—be really attractive." The end of Sabrina's sentence went unheard as the girl raced out of the rest room. "I know it doesn't seem like it, but I was trying to help!"

Sabrina sagged against the counter. She had had "being a real jerk" moments before, but blistering Maureen with brutal honesty had to be the jerkiest. "I really hate that phone."

* * *

Sabrina shifted impatiently in the cafeteria line. She just wanted to eat and run without talking to anyone. At least she didn't have to worry about getting into an uncomfortable situation with Harvey and Brad. The guys from auto shop were bagging it to finish up a project during lunch today.

When the line inched within reaching distance of the sandwich shelf, Sabrina grabbed a tuna on wheat and glanced ahead to the dessert case.

Gordy was ahead of her in line. Brow knit with indecision, he carefully studied the selections. He finally chose a cup of chocolate pudding.

"Come on, Gordy. Move it," Sabrina muttered softly.

Gordy started to set the cup on his tray and paused. He sniffed the rim of the cup, then poked his finger into the lumpy pudding. Wrinkling his nose, he quickly put the pudding back and grabbed a piece of apple pie.

Sabrina was opening her mouth just as the phone rang. "Gordy stuck his finger in that pudding!"

The phone went silent in mid-ring.

"Eew, gross!" The girl on the far side of Gordy made a face and moved away.

As all eyes turned to stare, Gordy froze, his face reddening with embarrassment. In the brief instant before he bolted out the door, he met Sabrina's gaze. "I never thought you were the kind of person who would hold a grudge, Sabrina."

He thinks I'm trying to get at him because he wouldn't loan me his science report!

Sabrina didn't even try to explain. Not even Gordy, scientific whiz and science fiction fan, would believe her cell phone had made her do it.

Employing some creative maneuvering and lame excuses, Sabrina managed to avoid Harvey and Brad most of the day. Her luck ran out in math. The phone wouldn't let her duck the class, and Harvey and Brad were in it.

Sabrina was already in her seat when Harvey and Brad arrived. Mrs. Chen came in right behind them as the bell rang.

"Hi, Sabrina." Harvey slid into the seat beside her. "Sorry about lunch, but Mr. Anderson wants Glen's car done by the end of the week."

"That's okay, Harvey." Sabrina smiled. "I understand."

"Hey, Sabrina." Brad's eyes swept right over Sabrina as he took the seat behind her and leaned across the aisle toward Harvey. "Five more minutes and I'm done for the day. Can't wait."

Harvey's eyebrow shot up. "You can't wait to go to the dentist?"

"It's just a cleaning appointment." Brad pulled a blue paper pass out of his math book.

Harvey touched the blue slip the school office issued when kids needed to leave school early for legitimate reasons. "Looks like you reached your mom to bring the excuse you forgot this morning."

Brad shook his head. "No, she wasn't home. I had to write an excuse and sign it myself."

Sabrina looked back, aghast. Brad completely misinterpreted her reaction.

"It's not like I'm faking a dentist appointment," Brad said defensively. "I really do have one."

And I really have a phone that won't stop ringing unless I tell! Sabrina turned her eyes to the front as the teacher called the class to order. She decided not to panic. Maybe forging a signature on an excuse for a real dentist appointment wasn't a wake-up call offense.

"Catch you later, Harvey." Brad scooped up his books and hurried to the front of the class, waving the pass.

Sabrina stiffened, counting off the seconds. At five, she thought the Silver Cloud SDE was going to let Brad get away with his minor transgression. At six, it rang.

"Wait!" Sabrina shot out of her chair as the teacher took Brad's pass. She didn't bother pulling out the phone. In the cafeteria it had hung up on its own after she humiliated Gordy. "Brad forged his mom's signature on the excuse!"

Brad and Harvey both snapped their heads around to stare at her.

"Is that true?" Mrs. Chen asked Brad.

Brad stopped glowering at Sabrina and nodded. "Yes, but I can explain."

"Let's discuss this in the hall." The teacher motioned Brad toward the door.

"I have a dentist appointment, Mrs. Chen. I just forgot my excuse this morning and—"

94

Sabrina fell back into her seat as the door closed behind them.

"I can't believe you did that, Sabrina!" Harvey's expression shifted between bewilderment and anger.

Sabrina just sighed. She couldn't explain her actions without telling the truth. Harvey wasn't as sharp as Gordy, but he wouldn't buy the phone cop story, either.

"How come you dislike Brad so much?" Harvey asked.

Sabrina responded with a shrug. *What am I going to say? That Brad makes me nervous because he might find out I'm a witch and I'll be munching cheese and exercising in a little metal wheel for the next hundred years?*

"You must have a reason," Harvey pressed. "I mean, I don't want to be the referee between you and Brad Friday night. I really want to watch the game."

Sabrina suddenly realized that she didn't dare go to the basketball play-off game with Harvey *and* Brad. She couldn't return the cell phone until Monday, and the risk of something going wrong was just too great.

"Then maybe you and Brad should go to the game without me, Harvey."

Harvey frowned. "I thought you wanted to go."

"I do," Sabrina replied. "I just don't want to go with Brad."

The truth hurts me more than it does you, Sabrina thought when Harvey's expression darkened.

"First you don't want Brad to go with us and then you do and now you don't again." Harvey exhaled with disappointed frustration. "Guess that settles it, though."

"Settles it how?" Sabrina tensed.

"I'll go with Brad." Shaking his head, Harvey turned away as Mrs. Chen came back into the classroom.

Sabrina dropped her chin in her hands. Sometimes being a witch in the mortal world was like being a fly in a hurricane. There was no way to win.

When the last bell rang, Sabrina dashed to her locker to pick up her books and head out to the park. She was anxious to leave school before anyone else fell prey to the cell phone's relentless wake-up calls. After getting what she needed, she slammed her locker closed. She gasped and fell back against it when she turned and almost ran into Dreama.

"What's wrong?" Dreama frantically touched her face. "Did I grow fangs or turn orange?"

"No, I just didn't expect to see you." Sabrina paused to catch her breath.

"Oh, good." Dreama sighed with relief. "I thought maybe my pep spell—"

"Don't tell me!" Sabrina snapped. Dreama hadn't quite mastered the rules regarding magical dos and don'ts in the mortal realm, and she didn't want to add the inept witch to the growing list of wake-up call victims. "Whatever you did, Dreama, I don't want to know. In fact, do yourself a big favor and stay away from me."

"I thought you liked me!" Dreama looked crushed.

"I do. That's the whole point!" Afraid something would go horribly wrong if she tried to explain, Sabrina fled down the hall.

"Fine, Sabrina!" Dreama called after her. "I've got plenty of other friends. I don't need you!"

That's the truth, Sabrina thought as she rushed outside. *With friends like me, you don't need enemies!*

With a heavy sigh, Sabrina collected her things and left the park. Thinking about everything that had happened that day only made her more depressed. The Silver Cloud SDE had transformed her into a one-girl police force with an inflexible agenda because the phone operated on the mistaken assumption that everything could be judged in terms of black and white. Neither extenuating circumstances nor causing greater harm affected its decisions about what was right and wrong.

And there's nothing I can do about it except become a hermit until Monday morning. That idea wasn't much comfort, but it was the only solution Sabrina had. She would have to go to school since the phone wouldn't let her skip, but as long as she didn't talk to anyone, everyone would be safe. However, she couldn't get out of working at the Clock Shop. Her aunts needed her help, and they were counting on her to show up.

Not a problem, Sabrina thought as she quickened her pace toward the store. People buying clocks wouldn't confide in a teenaged stranger, and Aunt Zelda rarely did anything wrong. Although Aunt

Hilda had a rebel's disregard for rules and regulations, she'd be too busy waiting on customers to get into trouble.

Sabrina relaxed, confident she could hang out at the Clock Shop for the next few days without having to worry about snitching on her aunts.

Chapter 11

Salem pretended to be asleep on the workbench when Hilda came into the storeroom. He was still irritated because she and Zelda had insisted on bringing him to the Clock Shop that morning. They had had the *nerve* to imply that *he* couldn't be trusted not to raid the refrigerator at home! The accusation was preposterous. *I can't* open *the refrigerator!*

"Where *is* that old pocket watch Zelda got from Teddy Roosevelt?" Hilda rattled the cans of miscellaneous clock parts on the shelves.

Did it play reveille? Cocking an ear, Salem kept his eyes closed as Hilda opened and closed the drawers in the workbench, then rifled through papers in the filing cabinet. He was pretty sure she was looking for the old, tarnished watch he had used as a hockey puck the last time they had brought him to the shop to keep him out of trouble.

"Just great," Hilda huffed. "I luck out and give a flyer to a collector, and now I can't find the *one* timepiece that's probably worth a small fortune!"

It's in a zillion pieces in a jar on the bottom shelf, Salem thought without remorse. Hilda, he decided, didn't really want to know that. Besides, it was Hilda and Zelda's fault he had smashed the watch when he had batted it into the door—about twenty times. *If they hadn't forgotten I was sleeping in the storeroom and gone home without me that night, I wouldn't have been playing storeroom hockey to keep my mind off food.*

FOOD! Famished, Salem moaned.

"Am I disturbing you?" Hilda asked.

"Yes, but I'm just the cat who's too weak from hunger to move, so don't mind me."

"I won't." Hilda lifted Salem to look under him.

"Hey!" Salem yelped. "If you won't feed me, you can at least respect my dignity!"

"Sorry." Hilda sighed as she set him down and mumbled again as she went back into the store. "Maybe he'd like that underwater watch with the tropical fish face that blows bubbles."

"There's an item any self-respecting collector would rather do without." Salem sat up and peeked through the door. Business had gone into an afternoon lull following the lunch rush. While Zelda rearranged the clocks on the shelves, Hilda tried to unload the fish watch on a small, wiry man wearing glasses and a bow tie.

"But it's a numbered limited edition," Hilda said.

"They only made ten thousand, five hundred and thirty!"

The man shook his head and tapped the paper he was holding. "This flyer said you had a pocket watch that Teddy Roosevelt once owned. That's the only reason I bothered to visit your common little establishment. I'd really rather not have to sue you for false advertising."

"Is it my fault that flyer doesn't know what it's talking about?" On the verge of losing her temper, Hilda paused to calm herself.

"Well!" The flyer sounded insulted. "*I* happen to know that that bubbling fish watch will be worth a *lot* ten years from now."

The man adjusted his glasses and squinted at the flyer. "How much is a lot?"

"A whole bunch!" The flyer lowered its voice. "But it's only fifty-nine fifty now."

"I'll take it." The man reached for his wallet.

"Thank you." Hilda winked at the man's flyer before she tossed it into the box behind the counter. She grinned and waved when Sabrina walked in. "Hi, Sabrina! You're just in time! Zelda and I could really use a break."

"Just let me stash my stuff, Aunt Hilda. Be right back."

Salem bristled as Sabrina entered the storeroom. "Well, if it isn't Sabrina the teenage snitch. Scratch that. I forgot I'm not talking to you."

"Salem?" Sabrina's books hit the bench beside

the cat with a loud thud when she dropped them. "What are you doing here?"

Lifting his chin, Salem turned his back and curled his tail over his front paws.

"Salem, I'm sorry about what happened last night." Sabrina's apology seemed genuine, but Salem was too hurt and hungry to care.

Tell it to my empty stomach! Salem flattened his ears.

"I *had* to tell Aunt Hilda you rigged the scale to win the bet because of this horrible phone!"

Salem hissed when Sabrina picked him up and turned him around to face her.

"Come on, Salem. Give me a chance to explain."

Salem covered his ears with his paws, but Sabrina didn't take the hint.

"The Silver Cloud SDE doesn't just give me wake-up calls when I do something wrong," Sabrina said softly. "It rings whenever anybody *around* me does something wrong!"

"Really? That could be interesting." Salem mentally chided himself for breaking his silence. Cat curiosity was a pain sometimes. "How many friends do you have left at school?"

"All the ones I didn't talk to or see today." Looking positively miserable, Sabrina scratched Salem behind the ears.

Salem purred. "That doesn't make up for a month of kibble and water, but it's a start. You wouldn't happen to have a stale cracker or two in your bag, would you?"

"No, but even if I did I couldn't give them to you." Sabrina rolled her eyes. "The phone would give me a wake-up call for aiding and abetting a known glutton who's going back on his word and cheating on his diet. Then I'd have to tell Aunt Hilda."

"Does this story get worse?" Salem asked.

"Of course. This is an Other Realm phone," Sabrina said matter-of-factly. "I can't get rid of it until the one-week free trial is up next Monday morning."

"You mean you can't sneak food to me to make up for setting me up to adjust the scale and then tattling on me for another *five* days!" Salem felt faint. "Couldn't Hilda and Zelda find a loophole in the contract?"

"I haven't asked because I didn't tell them about this dumb deal." Sabrina sighed. "They'd just lecture me about how nobody gets something for nothing and tell me I have to learn from my own mistakes. Like I don't already know that."

"I can relate." Salem nodded. "I've made a few dumb deals and mistakes in my life, too, not the least of which was getting busted and turned into a cat for trying to take over the world. Not my finest moment."

"So you won't tell?" Sabrina asked.

Salem hesitated. Sabrina hadn't deliberately gotten a cell phone that had turned her into an informer, but he didn't have to let her off the hook without a little payback. "Maybe, maybe not. I'll have to give the situation due thought and consideration before I decide if the revenge factor outweighs the potential benefits to me."

"I guess that will have to be good enough." Sabrina turned to leave.

"That's it? No counteroffer?"

"Meaning bribe?" Sabrina glanced over her shoulder. "Forget it. Definitely a Silver Cloud SDE no-no."

"What kind of motivation is *that* for keeping a secret?" When Sabrina just shrugged and left, Salem sprawled on his stomach in defeat. There was no point telling Sabrina's aunts about the phone if Sabrina didn't care!

Sabrina stepped behind the counter and tried to relax. She didn't expect the cell phone to object because she hadn't told her aunts about it. Apparently, signing a contract with Witch Wireless without parental permission wasn't a crime by the phone's definition.

"Did you have a good day?" Hilda shoved a cardboard file full of loose paper under the counter with her foot.

"I got through it." Sabrina smiled.

"So did we—barely. This is the slowest it's been all day." Zelda stood on the other side of the counter. She pushed her hair behind her ear and stole a guarded glance at Sabrina.

"What do you want me to do?" Sabrina tugged the hem of her long shirt to make sure it covered the cell phone in her back pocket.

"Take the money." Hilda gave the cash register an affectionate pat. "We'll do the rest."

"Okay." Sabrina's smile tightened when she realized Aunt Zelda was still staring at her. It was that look that meant her aunt wanted to talk about something but wasn't sure how to start. *And that usually means trouble for me.*

Zelda averted her gaze and began to straighten the items on the counter. "Did you see Willard today?"

"That sniveling snake that Zelda likes to date for reasons *I* will never understand," Hilda added.

"Uh, yes." Sabrina's insides knotted. *Did Mr. Kraft tell Aunt Zelda he's got me on expulsion watch? Or that I was suspended and now I'm not?* She felt like she was in the path of a runaway locomotive with no avenue of escape. No matter what her aunt wanted to know, she had to answer honestly.

"Dating is the problem," Zelda said.

"Dating?" Sabrina repeated.

"Exactly." Hilda held out her hands. "That's what I've been trying to tell you for months, Zelda. Willard is a loser."

"I'm beginning to think *I'm* the loser." Obviously agitated, Zelda began to pace in front of the counter. "When he calls he's always in a hurry and he hasn't asked me to go anywhere in two weeks!" Zelda frowned at Sabrina. "Have you noticed anything strange about Mr. Kraft at school?"

"*Everything* about Mr. Kraft is strange," Sabrina said.

"Understated, but accurate," Hilda agreed.

"Do you think he wants to dump me and just isn't man enough to say so?" Zelda asked.

"I certainly hope not!" Hilda gasped. "Imagine the disgrace if you were a Kraft dumpee and not the dumper!"

Sabrina quickly jumped in. "Mr. Kraft isn't going to break up with you, Aunt Zelda. He hasn't taken you anywhere because he's been working nights at Super Scoop. I saw him there last night."

"The ice cream place?" Hilda's initial surprise changed to impish delight. "He finally found a job that suits his personality. Soda jerk."

Zelda's face brightened suddenly. "Oh, that darling man. I've been hinting pretty broadly about taking a Caribbean cruise. I bet he's working an extra job to pay for it, isn't hc, Sabrina?"

Sabrina imagined the cell phone in her pocket getting ready to blast her. She knew what she had to do. Like Maureen, Aunt Zelda deserved to know the truth even if it hurt. "Uh, no, he's uh—actually, Mr. Kraft is working to buy a fishing boat."

"A boat!" Instead of being crushed, Zelda's face darkened with fury. "He wants to buy a *boat!*"

"That's what he said," Sabrina replied meekly.

"I don't know why that's making you so mad, Zelda, but I approve." Hilda faked an angry scowl. "How dare he!"

"Indeed!" Zelda exhaled and folded her arms. *"Before* he stopped taking me anywhere he was making me pay my own way! Including half the cost of gas!"

"Cheapskate." Hilda's gaze shot toward the front door. "Save your wrath for Willard later, Zelda. We've got customers!"

Thank goodness! As long as the store stayed busy, Sabrina could avoid any more close calls that might incite the zealous phone. Once they got home, she could use homework as an excuse to lock herself in her room. Isolation was the only way to protect her family and friends.

Sabrina stayed behind the counter as Hilda greeted a short woman wearing black leather with Biker Babe emblazoned on the back. Zelda assisted an elderly woman with a gaudy, flowered hat perched on her gray head.

"Excuse me." Salem jumped on the counter. "I got bored."

"You can watch, but no talking and no tricks," Sabrina cautioned him.

"Don't worry." Salem stretched out. "I'm not about to give you, the dauntless henchman of the phone police, another reason to totally mess up my life!"

"Quiet!" Sabrina hissed and turned her attention to the face-off in the front of the store. She would have loved a soothing cup of coffee from the coffeeshop right now, but she didn't want to bump into Josh there.

"But I want a wacky-witch-watch!" Biker Babe planted her hands on her hips and glared at Aunt Hilda.

Hilda matched the short woman's pose and jutted out her chin. "But you have to *buy* something first!"

"That's *not* what the flyer said!" the woman countered.

"Yes, it did! 'Get a wacky-witch-watch free with every *purchase*'!" Hilda hit the last word hard.

"That's what the *print* says, but that's *not* what the flyer said!" Biker Babe pulled a folded paper out of her jacket pocket and whipped it open with a snap of her wrist.

Puzzled, Sabrina did a double take and whispered to the cat. "Is that conversation making any sense to you?"

"No comment," Salem whispered back.

"Let me see that." Hilda ripped the flyer from the woman's hand. Her annoyed frown became an eye-rolling look of annoyed disgust. She reached into a basket and pulled out a thirteen-hour watch. "Here. Take it. Go ride!"

"Hey, thanks!" Grinning, Biker Babe sauntered out of the store.

Zelda left the old woman, who couldn't decide between a locket watch necklace and one that pinned on, to follow Hilda back to the counter. "What was that all about?"

"Defective flyer." Hilda handed the paper to Zelda.

Sabrina inhaled sharply when she saw the printed clock face transform into a 3-D animated face and speak in a rough voice. "Yo, lady! Stop by the store and take a wacky-witch-watch. They're free!"

"That's a magic flyer!" Hoping it wasn't so, Sabrina looked from one bewildered aunt to the other. "Unless this is some fantastic new mortal technology that nobody knows about except the lucky people—like you—that were chosen as a beta test group?"

"Get real!" Hilda chuckled as she leaned over the counter and dropped the flyer in the cardboard box. "Of course it's a magic flyer and, except for that dud, they've been working great!"

"Uh-oh," Salem said.

"Oh, no! Be right back!" Sabrina bolted into the storeroom and slammed the door closed. She crossed her fingers and closed her eyes, but the phone rang.

"This is a wake-up call."

"No, this is a calamity!" Sabrina couldn't believe it! Of all the people in this world and the Other Realm, her aunts were the last ones she expected to break the rules.

"This is a wake-up call!"

"I need to dial out!" Sabrina swallowed hard when the Silver Cloud SDE gave her a dial tone. She punched in the Other Realm emergency number, 119.

"Other Realm Police Department," a nasal voice said. "What is the nature of the emergency?"

"Magical infraction in the mortal world. My—"

The door opened, and Hilda and Zelda walked in. Salem darted between their legs and leaped onto the workbench.

"—aunts are using magic for personal gain!" Sabrina stared, horrified, as her aunts turned pale and vanished with two loud pops.

"What have I done?" Sabrina clutched the phone and shot a helpless glance at Salem.

"Well, let's see," he replied. "For starters, you just betrayed the only two people who could—"

Sabrina disappeared.

"—possibly help you." Salem blinked. "Now what am I supposed to do? I've been abandoned in the Clock Shop again with no food! And this time I don't have a hockey puck!"

Salem's whiskers twitched as he fought back a wave of panic. He had to get a grip!

"Hello." The elderly woman with the flowered hat shuffled through the storeroom door. A gold locket watch on a gold chain dangled from her white-gloved hand. She smiled at Salem and put two twenty-dollar bills on the bench in front of him. "I'll take this one."

Salem slammed his paw down on the money. *Deli, here I come!*

Chapter 12

I assume you have an explanation for this, Sabrina." Zelda stood beside Hilda in the defendant's box in an Other Realm courtroom.

"It can't be good enough, whatever it is," Hilda said.

The witches, warlocks, and assorted Other Realm beings in the jury box turned their heads in perfect sync to look at Sabrina.

Seated at a long table, Sabrina stared at her aunts across the brightly lit space between the wooden defendant's box, jury box, raised judge's bench, and defending attorney's table. Pitch-black darkness surrounded the illuminated arena where justice and injustice were dispensed on the whim of judge and jury in the Other Realm.

Sabrina withered under her aunts' hard gazes. "Well, I—"

"Order in the court!" A very tall, extremely thin

warlock rapped the floor with a long, wooden staff. Sporting the medieval page look in pointed shoes, tights, short balloon pants, long-sleeved white shirt, vest, and feathered cap, he had obviously been incorporated into the somber décor as festive relief.

"Which isn't working," Sabrina said under her breath.

"Shh!" The wizened little woman sitting beside Sabrina scowled at her through bifocal glasses poised on the tip of her long, hooked nose.

"Who are you?" Sabrina whispered.

A zipper appeared in place of the woman's mouth and disappeared an instant later. A feathered quill pen appeared in her gnarled hand. She scribbled on a three-foot-long yellow legal pad and turned it toward Sabrina.

Martha I-always-win Harding, prosecuting attorney, Sabrina read.

"All rise!" the bailiff announced.

Dazed by the unexpected turn of events and how quickly they were proceeding, Sabrina focused on her aunts as she stood up. Their attention was on the gorgeous young warlock who popped in to stand at the table beside the defendant's box. Impeccably dressed in a three-piece dark suit with a red power tie, he smoothed his dark hair and flashed her aunts a dazzling smile. His brilliant blue eyes pinged when he winked! *How come they got a cute lawyer and I got Miss Pickle Puss?*

"The Honorable Judge Maximum Sentence Logan presiding!" The bailiff pounded the floor with his staff as the judge billowed into the room in a cloud of blue smoke.

His Honor, a rotund, balding man with a bulbous red nose, beat the edge of his black robe with his gavel until it stopped smoldering. Shaking off the ashes, he huffed and puffed up twenty steps to take his lofty seat behind the bench.

"Be seated!" The bailiff paused as everyone but Sabrina's aunts sat down, then he coughed up the frog in his throat. Holding the green amphibian in one hand, he continued. "The court will now hear case number three million forty-eight V: *The Witches' Council v. Hilda and Zelda Spellman.*"

"Is this as serious as it looks?" Sabrina asked.

Martha zipped Sabrina's lips.

The bailiff whacked his staff on the floor so hard that it broke in two. The spindly man folded himself into a stooping position to retrieve the bottom half and fizzled out with his croaking frog.

"The charge is using magic for personal gain," Judge Logan bellowed. He inclined his head toward Hilda and Zelda. "How do you plead?"

The young attorney stood up. "My clients are guilty, Your Honor!"

"We are not!" Hilda stated emphatically.

"Well, actually we are," Zelda said, "but it wasn't deliberate."

"Right!" Hilda nodded.

"Very well." The judge turned to scowl at Martha. "Can you prove they *deliberately* used magic for personal gain?"

"Yes. I have hard evidence and an eyewitness." Martha stood up and pointed.

One of the Clock Shop flyers appeared in midair in the middle of the courtroom and launched into its sales pitch. "Guess what? You can get a thirteen-hour witch-watch *free* with every purchase at the Clock Shop!"

"Really?" The judge sat back. "I paid an outrageous price in rare spells for mine!"

"Your Honor!" Martha called his attention back to the matter at hand. "Although the defendants didn't order *magic* flyers from Duplicates Done for use in their mortal realm business, they continued to use the flyers to ensure sales *after* they discovered the advertising materials contained magical properties."

"True or false, Mr. Wickham?" the judge asked the young attorney.

"Absolutely true, Your Honor."

"Wait!" Hilda held up her hand. "Why are we in court? Whatever happened to punishment by 'dire circumstances' as an automatic result of using magic for personal gain?"

"*She* turned you in!" The judge pointed at Sabrina.

"Mmmmmphhh!" Sabrina nudged Martha and pointed to her zip-locked mouth. There had to be a way to save Aunt Hilda and Aunt Zelda from a fate worse than "dire circumstances." She didn't know what, but she hoped it would come to her once she started talking.

"Permission to unzip the witness, Your Honor." Martha stood ramrod straight with her hands primly clasped in front of her and her thin lips pressed in a smug smile.

The judge waved and Martha pointed. Sabrina jumped up as soon as the zipper dissolved.

"I didn't *want* to turn you in, Aunt Hilda and Aunt Zelda! I had to!" Sabrina pulled out the Silver Cloud SDE without missing a beat. "This *free* Witch Wireless cell phone has a wake-up call thingie that—"

Hilda and Zelda exchanged a glance, then threw up their hands.

"I guess you've heard about it, huh?" Sabrina sagged.

Hilda looked up. "It's one of the oldest scams in the book! It started with jungle drums and has worked its way through the Pony Express, the telegraph, and even extra wide, four-slot toasters!"

Zelda nodded. "You know some witches just love to play tricks on mortals and witches who live in the mortal world, Sabrina. They think it's *fun* to complicate our lives."

"I'd say this qualifies as a major complication," Hilda said.

"How was I supposed to know?" Sabrina knew ignorance was no excuse, but Nancy had not even given her a hint! *Whoa! Bright idea!* "Your Honor, I want to sue Witch Wireless for misrepresentation of their product!"

Mr. Wickham stepped toward Sabrina and held out his card. "I'd be more than happy to represent you."

"Forget it," Sabrina scoffed. "I'd rather have Martha."

"Excellent!" Martha pointed, and a thick file folder appeared in her hand. "Since Sabrina's lawsuit is relevant to the current case, I move to proceed immediately according to statute three, four, oh, nine—"

"Now?" The judge looked appalled. "I tee off in the Magician Invitational on Mars in fifteen minutes!"

"Well, if you drop the charges against my aunts, I'll drop my lawsuit," Sabrina said.

Martha stiffened. "Do you want a lawyer or not?"

"That depends on what the judge decides." Sabrina shrugged.

"How about a compromise?" Judge Logan rubbed his triple chin. "You drop the lawsuit and I'll forego any court action on the charges and let normal 'dire circumstances' stand."

Sabrina looked at her aunts. They both nodded. "Okay, Judge! It's a deal!"

The judge, the jury, the lawyers, and the courtroom disappeared, leaving Sabrina and her aunts standing in a small pool of fading light.

"How mad are you?" Sabrina asked.

"I'm very disappointed, Sabrina," Aunt Zelda said. "All this trouble could have been avoided if you had consulted us."

"Before *and* after you signed up with Witch Wireless," Hilda added. "But let's discuss it later. If we don't get back to Westbridge right now, we'll be back in court for inciting mass hysteria among mortals."

"Did you do something else I don't know about, Hilda?" Zelda's brow furrowed with worry.

"No," Hilda said. "We left Salem in charge of the Clock Shop!"

"Back so soon?" Salem was sprawled over his plate of fish and chips as Hilda, Zelda, and Sabrina came out of the storeroom.

"Not soon enough, apparently." Hilda raised the cat and pulled the plate out from under him. "How did you get this?"

"Funny thing about that." Stuffed after ingesting two cans of tuna and a box of dried shrimp treats, Salem didn't protest the loss of the half-eaten fish and chips. "People have a real soft spot for cats who are left all alone in a clock shop with no food or water."

"Please, tell me you didn't talk to them!" Sabrina clutched her cell phone to her chest. "I've lost enough friends and disappointed enough relatives today."

Zelda cast a stern glance at her troubled niece. "I have no sympathy, Sabrina. You made your deal and now you're going to have to deal with the problem."

"It's called tough love," Hilda said. "When is the contract up?"

"Not until Monday morning." Sighing, Sabrina slumped against the wall. "It's going to be a long week."

"Well, you don't have to worry about me." Salem smiled. "I didn't have to utter a word. All those customers just assumed I was hungry when I cried, panted heavily, and fell over."

"How many sales did we lose?" Zelda asked.

"None." Salem hit the button to open the cash register, which was stuffed with folded bills. "Since I couldn't make change, I'll take the overcharges as a tip."

"I don't think so." Zelda began to unfold the bills and insert them in the proper slots inside the cash drawer.

Annoyed, Salem swished his tail. "Aren't there laws against using cat labor without compensation?"

"I think you've been compensated enough." Hilda held up the plate and pointed to get rid of the leftovers.

Half the plate of fish and chips vanished. The other half fell on the floor.

"That wasn't up to your usual style," Salem observed dryly. His heart thudded with excitement. *If Hilda is losing her touch, maybe she'll be so upset she'll forget about my kibble and water diet!*

"What happened, Hilda?" Zelda dashed to the front of the counter.

"I don't know! I haven't noticed any knuckle cramps or muscle spasms." Hilda wiggled her finger. "Maybe we'd better close up shop until we figure it out."

"Good! I'm ready to go home and curl up on the sofa." Salem yawned.

"Here goes." Zelda fired a point at the front door to turn the Open/Closed sign. Instead of flipping over, it stopped halfway with the thin edge butted against the glass.

"Try that again." Hilda's voice wavered with an edge of hysteria.

Zelda pointed.

The sign turned another ninety degrees. It still wasn't lying flat against the window.

"Sabrina!" Hilda yelled. "Point!"

"I'm on it." Sabrina pointed at the pile of torn paper plate, fish, and chips on the floor. The mess vanished. She cast a point at the door. The sign finished its flip and flattened on the glass.

The toaster dinged in the back room.

Hilda and Zelda raced for the door, with Sabrina and Salem close behind.

"What is it?" Zelda asked when Hilda ripped a thick folded paper out of the toaster slot.

"It's a court document!" Hilda's hands shook as she unfolded the blue legal paper. "Judge Logan is charging us for court costs and lawyer fees!"

"Charging us what?" Zelda asked, her voice strained.

" 'There's no escape from dire circumstances,' " Hilda read aloud. She looked up, stunned. "Our magic will operate at only half power until the bill is paid!"

Zelda sank into the desk chair. "How long will that take?"

"It doesn't say." The paper slipped from Hilda's limp hand when she went into temporary spell deprivation shock.

"Well, half power is better than no power, isn't it?" Sabrina asked.

"Not much!" Zelda exclaimed. "It means we can't complete a spell! No matter how many times we point, the spell will only be half done and then half done again and on and on."

Cool concept, Salem thought. No matter how many times something was cut in half, there was always half left.

"We're grounded!" Hilda wailed.

"Look at the bright side," Salem said. "Now you'll know how *I* feel!"

Chapter 13

"**S**it down!" Salem stretched and dug his claws into Sabrina's bedspread. "All that pacing is wearing me out."

"I can't help it, Salem." Sabrina looked at the clock. She had decided to call Harvey ten times in the past ten minutes and had changed her mind nine. *Ten,* she corrected as she took her finger off the cell phone touch pad.

"I don't know why you're so upset about missing a basketball game." Salem resisted an urge to shred fabric and sheathed his claws. "I'm the one who's got *real* problems."

"What do you have to complain about?" Sabrina challenged. "Aside from being on a strict diet."

"Well, the monthly Alley Cat Screech and Howl Midnight Social is tonight, and I'm so weak from hunger I can barely mew," Salem replied. "So I'm not going because I don't want to embarrass myself in front of Trinket."

"Who's Trinket?"

"The Persian babe that moved in down the street last month," Salem sighed. "Why else would I make a bet with Hilda so I'd have extra incentive to get in shape?"

"Point taken, but you'll have another chance to howl next month." Sabrina straddled her desk chair and set the Silver Cloud SDE on the desk. She wrapped her arms around the chair back and rested her chin on the top. "This isn't just another basketball game. It's the play-off for the state championship," she said.

"Should I call Harvey?"

Salem's ears perked to attention. "Is he still talking to you?"

"Not as of three o'clock this afternoon, but maybe he's willing to forgive and forget getting detention because I told Mr. Kraft he was late for history class by thirty seconds." Sabrina's frown deepened. "Of course, he probably hasn't gotten over having to pay a ten-dollar library fine for overdue books because I talked Ms. Higgins out of letting him off easy, either."

Agitated because her social life was in shambles, Sabrina stood up and resumed pacing. "It's just not fair, Salem! It took me *three* years to move from being nerdy to being one of the cool kids. I've blown my whole image in four days!"

"Not surprising, since you've got a vigilante cell

phone for a sidekick." Salem stretched again and stood up.

Sabrina nodded. Not even a well-liked senior could get away with ruining friendships, breaking up couples, hurting feelings, and waging what appeared to be a determined campaign to fill up the detention room.

"I can clear a corridor and bring order to a classroom faster than Mr. Kraft," Sabrina said.

"A dubious achievement," Salem drawled, "but the old coot must be thrilled."

"Yeah. Thrilled because he's got an informant on the inside of the student body. Annoyed because I haven't done anything to get myself expelled." Sabrina sat on the edge of the bed. "You know you've totally bottomed out when *no* one will talk to you except the school principal."

"Don't worry!" Salem rubbed against Sabrina's arm. "When Zelda starts taking the old windbag's calls again and blasts him for moonlighting to buy a boat instead of taking her on a cruise, Mr. Kraft won't speak to you anymore, either."

"That's the only thing you've said that makes me feel better." Lying back, Sabrina stared at the ceiling. She had never felt so alone. Even Dreama had deserted her.

As Dreama's mentor in the mortal world, Sabrina usually omitted or downplayed Dreama's botched spells in her monthly progress report to the Witches' Council. This time she had been honest. Dreama had mixed a potion that was supposed to strengthen fingernails but instead turned fingernails into claws. She had flushed it down the drain in the chemistry lab and clogged the school plumbing. The fact that Dreama didn't know water would cause the potion to expand a thousand times its original volume was an honest mistake, but the Silver Cloud SDE wouldn't let Sabrina overlook it.

"So are you going to call Harvey?" Salem asked.

"No." Sabrina glared at the cell phone on the desk. "I'd probably spend most of the game arguing with the referee when he makes a bad call—even if it helps Amesbury! I don't think anyone at Westbridge would appreciate it."

"Probably not," the cat agreed.

"The best thing I can do for Harvey, the team, and the school is stay as far away from the game as possible." Sabrina had already decided to play it safe and spend Saturday and Sunday at home. Her aunts weren't even going to open the Clock Shop tomorrow because of the downsized power problem.

"That seems only fair since I can't go howl with Trinket tonight." The cat leaped to the window and parted the curtain with a heavy sigh. "I can only hope she doesn't fall for some scruffy alley cat."

"Sorry about that, Salem." Sabrina felt genuinely rotten for throwing Salem off his exercise program. "You wouldn't have lost your bet with Aunt Hilda if I hadn't adjusted the scale."

"Yeah, well, all's fair in love, war, and April Fools' jokes." Letting the curtain fall closed, Salem tried to yowl but managed only a kittenish mew. "Oh, that's pathetic!"

Sabrina dragged herself off the bed and pointed the Silver Cloud SDE into her pocket. "I'm off to see how much damage has been done by those half-spells. Care to join the patrol?"

"Of course!" Salem jumped down. "I need a few good laughs."

Sabrina's aunts had been using magic for ordinary tasks for so long that they pointed without thinking. Ordinarily that wasn't a problem, but now all their spells only half worked. To make matters worse, they kept casting test spells to see if their court bill had been paid yet. Sabrina could reverse the faulty spells with a combination of points reinforced with incantations. However, the rhymes had to be just right. After three days of periodic patrols through the house and a hundred fix-it spells, her rhymes were getting sloppy and lame.

Sabrina carefully opened her bedroom door. Salem hung back while she checked to make sure the hallway floor was still intact. *So far so good,* she thought as she stepped out and turned toward the stairs.

"They got my basket!" Salem cried.

Sabrina looked back. The top half of the large wicker basket sitting by the linen closet door was gone. She aimed her finger and recited:

> *Basket by the closet door,*
> *go back to how you were before.*

When Sabrina pointed, the woven reeds that formed the basket unraveled into a pile on the floor.

"I think that spell needs a little editing," Salem quipped.

"Everyone's a critic." Exhaling, Sabrina tried again.

Reeds assemble as before
with the basket all restored.

The basket became whole again when Sabrina pointed.

"Thank you!" Salem jumped onto the basket to make sure it was solid. "I love this basket. Good thing Hilda and Zelda's half spells aren't sealed."

"I'll say, or the whole house would be falling down around us." With her finger poised, Sabrina continued down the hall.

Sabrina paused at the top of the stairs. "Do you hear water running?"

Salem cocked his head. "Sounds more like a gusher. You don't think we struck oil in the dungeon, do you?"

"We couldn't be that lucky." Curious, Sabrina moved toward the bathroom. Water was seeping under the closed door. "This looks like a bad one, Salem."

"Uh oh!" Salem jumped back to avoid the advancing puddle and getting his picky feline feet wet.

Sabrina hesitated to think of an appropriate incantation. She started to speak as she raised her finger and opened the door.

> *Water, water everywhere,*
> *evaporate in—*

A wall of water burst out of the bathroom and swept Sabrina and Salem down the hall.

"Water! No! Anything but water!"

Sabrina grabbed the shrieking cat. Salem clung to her as the river washed them down the stairs. The white-water rapids dispersed throughout the house, leaving them drenched and sputtering in a shallow pool by the front door.

"Look at my beautiful fur!" Salem wailed. "I'm all wet! I hate being wet!" He paused. "Hey, swimming burns a lot of calories, right?"

A cough was Sabrina's reply.

"Oh, is it raining outside?" Hilda asked as she wandered out of the kitchen with a tall glass of lemonade. Half of her blond hair was neatly combed and curled, while the other half looked like somebody had glued clumps of straw to her head. She wiggled her toes, which stuck out of cut-off sneakers.

"You could say that." Sabrina squeezed water out of her shirt. "Who left the water running in the bathroom?"

"Oh, that's what that noise is!" exclaimed Hilda. "I forgot and tried to turn the water off with a point after I took a bath."

"Are you all right?" Zelda eyed Sabrina.

"I'm fine," Sabrina said, grinning as she stood up, "for someone who just bodysurfed a tidal wave down a flight of stairs holding a panicked cat."

"Would you mind . . . ?" Hilda began.

"Of course I will," said Sabrina. She dried her clothes, hair, and Salem with a quick point, then got to work rhyming.

> *Water, water everywhere,*
> *evaporate into the air.*

The puddles of water began to dry up with a flick of Sabrina's finger.

"I hope they get that court bill paid soon," Salem said.

"Me, too." Sabrina waved her finger to style her hair into a simple ponytail and sighed. "Let's go see what else we need to fix before—"

Thunder boomed.

"Were you expecting anyone?" Hilda asked Zelda.

Zelda shook her head. "Nobody from the Other Realm is going to visit two witches who aren't functioning at full power. It's much too dangerous."

Hilda frowned. "Then why is the linen closet—"

A bolt of lightning erupted from a dark cloud hanging below the ceiling. It cracked and sizzled to the ground between Sabrina and the library table, scorching a black spot into the polished wood floor. "Uh-oh."

"That was rather ominous." Salem leaped into

Sabrina's arms. "I think we're going to need an umbrella!"

Sabrina didn't argue. Realizing the cloud had formed because the air in the house was oversaturated with evaporated water, she pointed. Black umbrellas appeared in everyone's hands just as the cloud released a torrential rain.

"That was close." Salem snuggled against Sabrina, purring.

The doorbell rang.

"Now what?" Through the heavy rain, Sabrina saw Mr. Kraft peering through the narrowed, paned window beside the door. His eyes widened.

"Oh, why not." Since the principal had already seen the inside downpour, Sabrina opened the door. "Hi, Mr. Kraft!"

Dressed in his usual brown suit and vest, Mr. Kraft paused in the doorway and stared. "It's raining in your house."

"Sprinkler system broke," Sabrina explained. The Silver Cloud SDE rang in her pocket. "Actually, you're right. It's raining in my house."

The downpour eased off into a drizzle and stopped.

"Very funny." Rolling his eyes, Mr. Kraft stepped inside. "Is Zelda here?"

From the corner of her eye, Sabrina saw Hilda dash for the kitchen. Apparently, she didn't want Mr. Kraft to see her looking like a before and after picture in her one-sided mangled hairdo and severed sneakers.

Aunt Zelda shook her head and waved to signal Sabrina that she didn't want to see Mr. Kraft. If it wasn't for the cell phone in her pocket, Sabrina would have gladly told Mr. Kraft to take a hike because her aunt wasn't home. That wasn't an option.

"Yeah, she's here." Sabrina shrugged when Aunt Zelda sagged with exasperation. Over the past couple of days she had gotten very good at anticipating the wake-up calls, but it wasn't making her aunts very glad to be around her, either. *But unlike my friends, they're stuck with me.*

Zelda walked to the door with her black umbrella resting on her shoulder. She shook it, spattering Mr. Kraft, then folded it and set it aside.

"Don't you know it's bad luck to have an open umbrella in the house?" Mr. Kraft looked appalled.

"And how was I supposed to keep the rain off?" Zelda's innocent smile did not hide the edge of bitterness in her tone.

"I don't think I want to answer that question," Mr. Kraft said.

Intrigued, Sabrina sat down on the damp stairs with Salem in her lap. It wasn't very often she got a chance to watch Mr. Kraft grovel, and she wanted a ringside seat.

Folding her arms, Zelda didn't mince words. "What are you doing here, Willard?"

"Well, I know I haven't been very attentive lately." Mr. Kraft shoved his hands in his pockets and stared at his feet. "But I thought maybe you might like to go with me—"

Zelda's posture started to relax.

"—to the school basketball game tonight." Mr.

Kraft looked up and smiled. "Westbridge is in the play-offs. It should be really exciting."

Sabrina pouted, indulging in a little self-pity because she couldn't go to the game. *Like Aunt Zelda cares whether the Scallions beat the Amesbury Indians.*

"I've got a better idea." Zelda turned the startled man around and pushed him out the door. "Go by yourself. I'm not going to be a weekend boating widow!"

Mr. Kraft glanced back. His demeanor and tone were both condescending. "I'll call you when you're not quite so upset."

Zelda stiffened as Mr. Kraft walked away, then she suddenly cast a point. "Take that!"

Oh, boy! Sabrina ran to the door and smothered a laugh with her hand.

Half a neon sign flashed on Mr. Kraft's back.

" 'Kick I'm'?" Sabrina looked at Zelda, puzzled.

"There're two words missing! It's supposed to say 'Kick me I'm bad.' " Zelda stamped her foot.

"Not a problem. The sign's gotta go." Sabrina leveled her finger at Mr. Kraft's receding back and spoke in a rush to beat the cell phone to the punch.

> *Although the sentiment's on track,*
> *remove the sign on Willard's back.*

Zelda frowned when the green letters blinked out. "You're no fun anymore, Sabrina."

"Believe me, I'm not ecstatic about being the

family moral barometer," Sabrina replied. "I can't wait to send the Silver Cloud SDE back on Monday morning."

"Sabrina!" Hilda shouted from the kitchen. "I just forgot and pointed to get my anvil down from the attic!"

Zelda, Salem, and Sabrina all jumped back when Hilda's anvil appeared in midair before them. It hung suspended for a split second, then crashed onto the floor.

"Well, it made it halfway," Salem said.

Sabrina nodded. It was going to be a very long weekend.

Chapter 14

Monday morning at exactly eight o'clock, Sabrina tossed the Silver Cloud SDE into the linen closet and slammed the door. Thunder boomed. Lightning flashed, and the dreaded cell phone was on its way back to Witch Wireless.

"So long and good riddance!"

Feeling like a great weight had been lifted off her shoulders, Sabrina dashed downstairs with a bounce in her step and a smile on her face. Not even Aunt Hilda's half-baked blueberry muffins could dampen her high spirits today.

"I'm free!" Sabrina burst into the kitchen with her arms raised in victory.

Her aunts sat at the table wearing bathrobes. Zelda gave her a limp wave and absently sipped tea.

Hilda raised her head off her folded arms and yawned. The circles under her eyes were so dark that it looked like she had put makeup on upside down. "How can you be so chipper so early, Sabrina? I'm still half asleep."

"Did you try to make a sleeping potion or a wake-up tonic?" Zelda asked.

"Aunt Zelda! I don't ever want to hear the word *wake-up* again!" Sabrina noticed that the back door was half closed and whipped up a quick rhyme.

Here's a clue! It's ajar!
Close the door to our backyard!

The door slammed closed as Sabrina pointed and settled into a chair.

"I don't know what's worse, Zelda." Hilda propped her head up with her hand. Her heavy eyelids drooped. "Not being able to work a whole spell or listening to Sabrina's chants."

"Don't be so critical, Hilda." Zelda patted Sabrina's hand. "I thought her incantation to clear the glacier out of the laundry room was rather clever."

"I just wanted an ice pack for a headache," Hilda said. "Since when does ice pack get translated as iceberg?"

"That's the first definition in the dictionary," Zelda explained patiently.

"That was a good chant, though, wasn't it?" Sabrina grinned. " 'Glacier growing like a fungus, we don't want you here among us.' "

Hilda groaned. "A little mercy for the weary would be nice."

Sabrina decided to tone down her bubbly mood

out of sympathy for her aunts' distress. Considering they had gone five days without being able to use their magic properly, they weren't nearly as touchy as she might have expected.

"Okay, I'll stop chanting as soon as you stop casting half spells, Aunt Hilda. Besides, I have to go to school so I won't be home to fix stuff today." Sabrina's eyes narrowed. "Are you going to the Clock Shop?"

"Not until our powers are restored." Zelda sighed. "We can't really afford to lose any sales, but it's just too risky under the circumstances."

"What about all those flyers that are still out there?" Sabrina asked.

"The magic wore off the flyers on Friday," Zelda explained. "When we do open again, it will be back to business as usual."

"Which means no business as usual," Hilda mumbled.

"Bummer. What's for breakfast?" When both women gave her a you've-got-to-be-kidding look, Sabrina took the hint and pointed up bakery fresh muffins and O.J. for everyone. "Where's Salem? I haven't seen him all morning."

"Moping somewhere." Zelda held up her teacup, and Sabrina refilled it with full-strength Earl Gray. "He's not being a very good sport about having to stay on his kibble diet."

"I don't blame him, actually." Sabrina picked up her muffin and set it down again. "The truth is Salem *had* lost the two pounds. If I hadn't tricked him into exercising all morning, he wouldn't have gotten so hungry he couldn't tough it out until six o'clock. It's really my fault he lost the bet."

"Is that the Silver Cloud SDE talking?" Zelda eyed Sabrina over the rim of her cup.

"No, that's me being honest on my own," Sabrina said. "The Silver Cloud SDE is history, I'm happy to say."

"I'm happy to hear it." Hilda shook her head to clear it and sat up. "I suppose I could be a little lenient on Salem. The past seven days have been a little weird."

"Does that mean you won't hold him to the bet?" Sabrina nodded to prod her aunt.

"Sure." Hilda yawned. "I'm tired of fighting—"

"Yes! Woohoo!" Salem raced into the kitchen and leaped onto the counter. "I'll have tuna in spring water, a Bavarian cream doughnut, a vanilla shake, and a box of dried shrimp treats. Better throw in a large bottle of antacid tablets for good measure."

Sabrina pointed at Salem's bowl. "I think you'd better settle for King Kitty Salmon Delight until your stomach adjusts."

"If you insist." Salem dug in.

Sabrina smiled. As soon as her aunts had full use of their magic again, everything would be back to normal—almost. She still had to salvage her shattered reputation and try to win her friends back, which wouldn't be easy, since no one was talking to her.

* * *

As Sabrina walked through the halls of West-bridge High, everyone in her path turned away or ducked out of sight. She pretended not to notice or care. Eventually, her reign of terror would be forgotten. In the meantime, she had to stay calm and play it cool. The first thing she had to do, though, was make up with Harvey.

And luck is with me, Sabrina thought when she saw Harvey opening his locker. Brad was not there. She wasn't sure what approach would work best, so she opted for the familiar. *Act like nothing's wrong and go from there.*

"Hi, Harvey! How's it going?"

"Hi, Sabrina." Harvey cast a quick glance over his shoulder, then turned back to his locker. He didn't smile. Bad sign.

"So—how was the game?" Sabrina suddenly realized she had been so busy cleaning up after her aunts' half spells all weekend that she didn't even know who won.

"Lousy. Amesbury whomped us sixty-eight to forty." Harvey shrugged. "You didn't miss anything."

"I missed you," Sabrina blurted out.

"Yeah, well, I'd better get to class. I don't want to be *late* again."

Harvey's implied accusation hit Sabrina hard, especially because she was guilty. Somehow, she had to explain her behavior so Harvey wouldn't be mad at her.

"Harvey, wait."

"I'm kind of in a hurry, Sabrina." Harvey looked down the corridor, but he didn't walk away.

"I'm sorry the Scallions lost, but I just, well—I just, uh—thought you and Brad needed a guys' night out. Without me hanging around being a girl getting in the way of the guy bonding thing."

When Harvey frowned in typical Harvey confusion, Sabrina was sure she had made a breakthrough. Then she heard a phone ring.

In her bag.

"Your phone's ringing," Harvey said.

"My phone? Oh, yeah!" Heart pounding, Sabrina opened her bag. The Silver Cloud SDE was nestled inside between her makeup kit and a memo pad. She didn't know why it had returned, but this time she couldn't afford to waste time figuring it out. "Sorry, Harvey. Gotta go!"

Sabrina ran for the nearest rest room.

"Aunt Hilda! Aunt Zelda!" Sabrina popped into the kitchen. Her aunts weren't there, but Salem was stretched out on the counter.

"Why aren't you at school?" The cat burped.

"The phone's back!" Panicking, Sabrina rushed over to the cat. "Why?"

The phone rang again.

"I don't know, but if you hurry you can catch Hilda and Zelda before they pop to the Clock Shop." Salem belched again.

"Does that mean they're running on full power again?"

"Apparently. The cheese soufflé with a side of caviar Hilda pointed came out perfect." Salem moaned. "Before you go, I could really use some antacid tablets."

After pointing up a bottle for Salem, Sabrina raced through the house. Her aunts were upstairs in Zelda's bedroom trying on different outfits.

"How come you're skipping class, Sabrina?" Zelda eyed her reflection in a full-length mirror, then pointed. A tailored gray pants suit was replaced by a flowered print dress that was ideal for a gorgeous spring day. "What do you think, Hilda?"

"I think it's great to be a witch with powers that work!" Hilda pointed to change her dangling diamond earrings into plain gold studs.

"The phone's back!" Desperate, Sabrina pointed to flip the mirror so she could have her aunts' undivided attention. "The contract for the one-week free trial was up this morning! So why did it come back again?"

"Well, you obviously haven't gotten the message." Hilda looked past Sabrina to Zelda. "Want to do lunch in Paris?"

Chapter 15

This has got to be one of the worst weeks in my whole life!" Sabrina vented her frustration as she popped back into a stall in the rest room at Westbridge High. She had no idea what "message" she was supposed to get beyond the continuing wake-up calls. Her aunts had told her she'd have to figure it out, but she didn't have a clue.

"Sabrina? Is that you?"

Sabrina recognized Maureen's voice. She really didn't want to talk to anyone, but she couldn't snub Maureen after the hard time she had given the girl. Stuffing toilet paper into her bag to muffle the annoying phone, she stepped out and gawked. "Maureen? Is that you?"

"Yeah, it's me!" Maureen raised her arms and turned in a circle. "Is this what you meant?"

Pleasantly surprised, Sabrina nodded. Maureen had dyed her hair to a natural dark brown color and had removed the diamond from her tooth. If she was wearing makeup, she had applied it with a light touch, just enough to enhance her large, brown eyes. She was wearing a stylish, loose sweater—no glittering sequins—over jeans.

"You look great, Maureen! I'm so impressed."

"Really?" Maureen giggled. "Well, I have you to thank for the new me. It took a couple of days, but your message finally came through loud and clear."

"Then you're more perceptive than I am." Sighing, Sabrina set her bag on the sink. *What message am I missing?*

Maureen peered inside Sabrina's bag and frowned. "There's someone talking on your cell phone. I wish I had one. Cell phones are so cool."

"Believe me, Maureen, I was a lot happier before I got one." And a lot cooler, too, Sabrina realized. Having a cell phone hadn't enhanced her image like she wanted. The Silver Cloud SDE had driven her to the bottom of the "cool" pool. "Here's some more advice if you want it, Maureen."

"Sure!" Clasping her books to her chest, Maureen leaned forward in rapt attention.

"Having cool stuff doesn't make anyone cool," Sabrina said. "It's who you are and what you do that really counts, and anyone who doesn't understand that is *not* cool. Got it?"

"Absolutely." Grinning, Maureen turned to leave and looked back. "Did I tell you I've got a date with Danny Evans next Saturday?"

"Now *that's* cool!" After Maureen left, Sabrina

took a long, hard look at herself in the mirror. She didn't know if anyone but Maureen would ever think she was cool again, and she didn't really care. She had alienated all her friends, her boyfriend, and her boss because she just had to have a silly status symbol. Now she just wanted everything to be okay with everyone again.

"And get rid of this stupid phone!" Sabrina opened her bag and blinked. The Silver Cloud SDE was gone. "So what was the message? How to be cool without being a jerk?"

No phone rang to provide a handy answer.

"I think I'll quit while I'm ahead." Grabbing her bag, Sabrina rushed into the hall to start putting the pieces of her life back together. However, as though fate couldn't stand the idea of things going right for more than five minutes, she ran into Mr. Kraft outside the door.

"Why aren't you in class?" Mr. Kraft reached into his pocket.

He has to be the fastest pen and detention pad in the east, Sabrina thought wryly.

"Major personal crisis, Mr. Kraft. I know that's no excuse, but—what's that?" Sabrina was surprised when he pulled a slip of paper from his pocket instead of a detention pad.

"It's a bonus check from the school board." Mr. Kraft sighed heavily. "And as much as it pains me to say so, I have you to thank for it."

"Yeah?" Sabrina wondered if she had just dropped into an alternate universe without knowing it.

"Yes. Finding out I was working a second job prompted Mrs. Markum to reevaluate how much they're paying me and determine it wasn't enough." He fought back a smile. "I'll probably get a substantial raise when they renew my contract for next year."

"That's terrific." Sabrina was genuinely pleased for him. "Is it enough to pay for your boat?"

"Enough to cover the down payment with a little left over." Mr. Kraft put the check back into his pocket and scowled. "Now tell me how I can get your Aunt Zelda to like me again and I won't give you detention."

"Easy. Take her out to dinner at an expensive restaurant and pick up the check."

By lunch, Sabrina had apologized to dozens of kids, including several she probably *hadn't* gotten into trouble during her wake-up call rampage. Most of them, including Gordy and Dreama, had shrugged it off with no hard feelings. Dreama had been the easiest to convince. Being a witch who suffered the consequences of misused magic all the time, she totally understood the Other Realm cell phone problem. Sabrina just hoped Harvey would be as forgiving.

Harvey and Brad were already eating when Sabrina walked off the cafeteria line with her tray. She couldn't tell them the truth about why she had begged off going to the game because she couldn't tell Brad he was a witch hunter that threatened her security as a teenage witch. So maybe she should just follow through with her original plan: act like nothing was wrong and hope for the best.

"Hey, guys!" Sabrina smiled when she reached the table. "Got room for one more?"

"We've always got room for you, Sabrina." Harvey pulled out the chair beside him. "I was just telling Brad what you said this morning."

"What was that exactly?" Sabrina asked.

"About doing guy stuff together." Harvey grinned. "It's totally cool that you don't get upset or jealous just because there's some things guys want to do with just guys."

"Well, you know me. I'm just brimming with understanding." Sabrina caught Brad staring at her and smiled back in spite of a sudden surge of apprehension.

"Then you won't mind if Harvey goes camping with me this weekend?" Brad held her gaze, daring her to object.

"Mind? No! Go! Have fun with the bugs and other creepy critters!" Sabrina didn't want to spend another weekend without Harvey, but she owed Brad one. It was also a small price to pay to see Harvey smile at her again.

Sabrina went directly to the coffeehouse after school. Needing to catch her breath, she paused outside the door and peered inside. She really wanted to apologize to Josh for being rude to the owner's daughter and get it over with, but the place was packed. *Probably not a good time,* she thought as she watched Josh race from one table to another picking up dirty dishes.

Disappointed, Sabrina headed back down the sidewalk. Josh looked too busy and harried to interrupt just so she could clear a guilty conscience. She wasn't even sure he would welcome her back as a customer.

"Sabrina! Wait!"

Surprised to hear Josh call her name, Sabrina stopped dead and spun around. She was even more surprised to see him running toward her. "Hi, Josh."

"Where do you think you're going?" Wearing a rumpled, stained apron and obviously frazzled, Josh frowned when he stopped before her.

"I didn't think you had time to talk, so I was going home."

"Home? The place is mobbed!" A sudden smile broke out on Josh's handsome face. "But you're right, I don't have time to talk because I can't find any decent help. I've hired and fired three waitresses since you left."

"That many? Did they insult Evelyn, too?"

Josh laughed. "No, only you had the nerve to do that. She treats everyone like a lower life form, so it's about time somebody tried to knock her down a peg or two. Not possible because she's such a spoiled brat, but at least you had the guts to give it a shot."

"Not the most brilliant career move I've made lately, though," Sabrina said. "You fired me."

"Yes, I did." Nodding, Josh ran his fingers

through his tousled hair. "And I can hire you again, if you want your old job back."

"You want me back?" Sabrina started to gush with joy, then frowned. "What about Evelyn's father?"

"I haven't heard from him," Josh said, "but if I had, I would have told him that you were totally justified. He probably agrees, which is why he didn't call. So what do you say?"

"Where's my apron?" Sabrina beamed, pleased and astounded.

"Right where you left it. So what are you standing here for?" Josh waved her toward the door. "Let's go. There's ten more tables that need to be bussed."

"I'll be there in a minute." Sabrina fished a quarter out of her pocket and gestured toward a row of pay phones down the block. "My aunts are expecting me at the Clock Shop. I have to call so they don't worry."

"Two minutes." Josh started to leave, then hesitated. "Why don't you use your new cell phone?"

"I turned it back in to the company." Sabrina rolled her eyes. "It just wouldn't stop ringing!"

As Josh headed back inside scratching his head, Sabrina dashed to the pay phones, deposited her quarter, and dialed. "Hey, Aunt Hilda! How's it going?"

"It's been another dynamite day," Hilda said with enthusiasm. "We just sold all the wacky-witch-watches to Biker Babe's biker buddies."

"So the Clock Shop is saved for another month!" Zelda yelled in the background.

Looks like everyone's fortunes are changing for the better today, Sabrina thought. She quickly told

Hilda her good news about going back to work and the cell phone going back to Witch Wireless permanently. "You don't need me there, do you? Josh is swamped and wants me to start five minutes ago."

"No problem, Sabrina. We'll celebrate when you get home."

Sabrina hesitated, wondering if she should take advantage of the rosy circumstances while she could. Since everything else had worked out for the best, she decided to go for broke. "What are the chances of getting a regular cell phone? For my birthday maybe? Or now that I'm working again, I could save up."

"We'll talk about it," Hilda said, "after you pay the hundred and seventeen dollars you still owe on your long-distance bill."

Sabrina hung up and burst out laughing. After a long week of trauma, trial, and tribulation everything was back to normal. With or without a cell phone, she was totally glad that some things never changed.

"Sabrina!" Josh hollered out the coffeehouse door. "Are you coming or do I have to fire you again?"

"Coming!" Sabrina ran. She felt so good she didn't even care if she had to clean the rest rooms again. Josh didn't know it, but she had a mighty-magic-finger-cleaner that did all the dirty work for her. "Sometimes you just have to take advantage of being a teenage witch."

About the Author

Diana G. Gallagher lives in Minnesota with her husband, three dogs, three cats, a parrot and a guinea pig called Red Alert. She has three grandsons called Jonathan, Alan and Joseph. When she's not writing she enjoys walking her dogs, pottering in her garden and playing the guitar.

Diana has written a variety of fiction for children and teenagers as well as authoring various adult titles too. She is also an award-winning artist and is a great fan of Irish and folk music.

Don't miss out on any of Sabrina's magical antics — conjure up
a book from the past for a truly spellbinding read . . .

#35 Pirate Pandemonium

Sabrina realised she couldn't possibly know everything
about her aunts, who have lived for hundreds of years. But
she never imagined that Aunt Zelda spent a summer as a
buccaneer sailing the high seas.

When Aunt Zelda's old friend, pirate Edwin 'Eddie' Peas,
pops up from the Other Realm seeking her help to rescue his
kidnapped crew, it's all hands on deck for Sabrina and
Salem. But sailing on Eddie's ship, Screamin' Mimi, is hardly
the luxurious Caribbean vacation Sabrina had envisioned . . .

In order the save the captives from King Feargus II of
Ootnanni, they must find the mssing treasure before they
too, end up in the stomach of Ol' Agnes, the giant sea
monster.

Runaway Bride

False Pretences

Out of Bounds

Making Waves

Illusions of Evil

Flirting with Danger

Fatal Attraction

Till Death Do Us Part